PUCKING EVER AFTER

VOLUME ONE

EMILY RATH

Fall in love a thousand ways

EMILY RATH BOOKS

WWW.EMILYRATHBOOKS.COM

This is for you, readers.

You've changed my fucking life, and I'm so profoundly grateful.
You wanted more Price Family. Here you go.

AUTHOR'S NOTE

If you're here, it means you've read **THAT ONE NIGHT** and **PUCKING AROUND** and you loved them. Right? RIGHT?? If you haven't read those books yet, you reeeeeally need to do that first. Otherwise, this little volume of bonus content won't do much for you.

As I build out the Jacksonville Rays universe, I want to have plenty of content to offer my readers during the in-between times of the main book releases. **PUCKING EVER AFTER** is one way I can give you more Rays in smaller bites!

This is just Volume One. Meaning there _**will**_ be more volumes. Oh, and I do take requests (sort of). Enjoy!

XO,

Emily

TROPES, TAGS, & CONTENT WARNINGS

TROPES

Happily ever after; hockey romance; bonus content; why choose

TAGS

Babies, happily ever after, hockey, why choose, Team Price, jam nipples, the most unconvincing straight man you've ever met, Super Jake, DVP, net kink, Price Family Storage Closet, put a dollar in the swear jar, Poseidon Price

CONTENT WARNINGS

This book contains themes that may be distressing to some readers including: depictions of pregnancy, mentions of non-life-threatening post-birth hemorrhage, and mention of a newborn who needs time in a NICU for a mild case of jaundice.

This book also contains detailed two-, three-, and four-person sex scenes that include elements of impact play, choking, double vaginal penetration, degradation/praise, and public sex.

STAR SIGNS:

- RACHEL: Cancer (water): intuitive, emotional, guarded
- ILMARI: Aries (fire): bold, ambitious, temperamental
- JAKE: Taurus (earth): focused, sensual, steadfast
- CALEB: Sagittarius (fire): adventurous, adaptable, blunt

MEET THE RAYS

PLAYERS

Davidson, Tyler (#65): backup goalie
DeGraw, Hunter (#1): starting goalie
Fields, Ethan (#94): forward
Gerard, Jean-Luc "J Lo" (#6): defenseman
Hanner, Paul (#24): defenseman
Karlsson, Henrik (#17): forward
Langley, Ryan (#20): forward
Morrow, Cole (#3): defenseman
Novikov, Lukas "Novy" (#22): defenseman
Perry, David "DJ" (#13): forward
Price, Ilmari "Mars" (#31): starting goalie
Price, Jake (#42): defenseman, Captain
Walsh, Cade (#10): forward

COACHES

Andrews, Brody: Assistant Coach
Johnson, Harold "Hodge": Head Coach
Tomlin, Eric: Goalie Coach

TEAM SUPPORT

Gordon, Jerry: Assistant Equipment Manager

Jones, Cody: Equipment Tech

Price, Caleb: Head Equipment Manager

MEDICAL SUPPORT

Jacobs, Hillary: Team Nurse

O'Connor, Teddy: PT intern

Price, Rachel: Assistant Director of Physical Therapy

Tyler, Scott: Team Doctor

OPERATIONS/MANAGEMENT

Francis, Vicki: Operations Manager

Ortiz, Claribel: Social Media Manager

St. James, Poppy: Public Relations Director

CHAPTER BLURBS

1. Häagen-Dazs (Jake)

This was a fan request! Sam of @rain.books.and.tea wanted to see Jake's super power in action. Enjoy this cute moment of Jake picking out Ilmari's ice cream flavor.

2. Emergency Contact (Rachel)

Filling out medical paperwork becomes a bit of an issue when the Fearsome Foursome each realize who the others listed as their emergency contact.

3. Up in the Air (Rachel)

It's 3:00am and the team is flying high somewhere over the skies of the Midwest. Rachel should be sleeping. Determined to help her relax, Ilmari takes matters into his own hands.

4. IKEA (Ilmari)

The last thing Ilmari wants to do after a busy day is get dragged to IKEA. Little does he know, his day is about to get a lot more interesting.

5. Paternity Test (Rachel)

Rachel is in the hospital, waiting to get discharged, when the nurse arrives with some exciting news.

6. King of the Ice (Caleb)

Caleb and Ilmari watch Jake lead the Rays to a major victory and Caleb can't help but remind Jake who's really king of the ice.

1

HÄAGEN-DAZS

JAKE

"I need to grab some deodorant." Without waiting for my response, Caleb wanders off the moment we step through the sliding doors into Publix.

"Hey—meet me in frozen!" I shout at his back.

He doesn't respond, head down as he checks his phone.

Asshole. He always disappears and then it takes me like ten minutes of prowling the aisles to find him again. Why can't he just stay by my side? We only came in here for one thing. I swear, next time I'm gonna put Poseidon's leash on him and give him a tug whenever he tries to wander off.

Speaking of the dog, he's out waiting in the car with the window cracked. And I'm itching to get to Seattle. I wanna make this detour quick. I snatch up a green shopping basket by the handles and head in the opposite direction of Cay, down towards the ice cream aisle.

It feels like it's been days since I've seen her, instead of only hours. We crossed paths a few times at the practice rink this morning. She watched me doing some drills with the other defensemen out on the ice. Later, she flashed me a flirty wink in the gym that had me adjusting myself over by the elliptical.

But then Mars had to offer her a ride home while I was still tied up with my strength and conditioning coach. Of course, he didn't mean *our* home. You know, the one where she *lives*. With *me*. Cay and I got home to find the house empty. Sy was whining and doing his pee dance by the front door.

Well, fuck that. I'm not spending the whole night crawling out my damn skin needing my girl. I don't care that she's off fucking Mars right now. I'm not jealous about the sex. He just wanted time alone with her. As much as I like sharing her, I need my time alone with her too.

But even with his magical Viking cock, he can only go for so many rounds, right? The solo sex is one thing, but he doesn't just get to keep her locked up all night. She's mine too. She's *ours*. Our Finnish friend is gonna learn to share, or I'm about to become a major pain in his sculpted ass.

Rachel brought this on herself when she gave me his address. And with the email that just pinged on my phone fifteen minutes ago, I now have the perfect excuse. We'll watch game day footage at Ilmari's house. It's foolproof. He can't say no, not when I'm bringing ice cream to share. Their twosome is about to become a foursome.

Well...technically a fivesome, because Caleb made me bring the dog too.

I make a sharp right turn down aisle 12. I'm actually excited. I haven't had a chance to flex my super power in a while. With Rachel, it was almost too easy. Of course, she's a sorbet girl. She likes to think she's cutting the calories with sorbet. And since it's fruit flavored, instead of chocolate or caramel, she doesn't have to feel as bad about pounding an entire pint in one sitting.

The only tricky thing is that her tastes change. Does she want something sweet tonight, like a cool refreshing raspberry? Or a tart lemon? What does post-sex Rachel need? Going with my gut, I snatch up a lemon sorbet, and drop it in the basket. Then I stand before the wall of Häagen-Dazs.

"Game time," I mutter, looking over the labels.

I pluck out a pint of Mint Chip for Caleb from the bottom row. If the special edition Peppermint Bark was available now, I'd be reaching for that instead. But you can always count on that weirdo to want mint in his coffee *and* his ice cream.

The funny thing is that he doesn't like mint gum. Or mint toothpaste. He prefers cinnamon for his gum. And he uses that weird toothpaste with the baking soda that makes your teeth feel all grainy. It's gross. Give me peanut butter in my ice cream and mint in my toothpaste.

Eyeing the Chocolate Peanut Butter one row up from the Mint Chip, I grab a pint for myself and add it to the basket. Now comes the hard part. Mars Kinnunen. Usually my super power is almost like a reflex. I just *know*...you know? Tess walked in my house the other week and before she even spoke a word, I was ready to offer her a pint of Ben & Jerry's Cherry Garcia.

Our team captain, Sully, is a total Rocky Road. No brand names though. Price over quality. He wants the cheapest, most freezer-burned Rocky Road you can find. I swear, that man has forgotten how to live.

And Morrow tries to play it off like he's so laid back and cool, but I know he's a White Chocolate Raspberry Truffle guy.

Novy is lactose intolerant. He had cheese on a pizza once, and I was the unlucky asshole sharing a hotel room with him. I almost made him sleep in the bathtub. So, no ice cream for him.

I smirk, glancing to the left of the Häagen-Dazs case, to see a box of banana pops on the top shelf. Yeah, Novy is a kid's popsicle. Cheap, sticky sweet, but reliable and satisfying.

None of this helps me now, of course. I'm not here picking out popsicles for Novy or ice cream for Tess. I need to focus. What kind of ice cream would Mars want? My eyes scan the wall of flavors as I mutter under my breath. "Nothing fruity...and nothing with cookies..."

He just doesn't seem like the type to want fruit in his ice cream. And he's like Cay with the no drinking thing, so the special edition boozy flavors are out too.

As I deliberate, Caleb saunters up behind me, dropping deodorant, floss, and suntan lotion into the basket. "You ready to go?"

"Shut up," I murmur, eyes locked on the case. It's floating right in front of me. I can almost reach out and snatch it from the air, that illusive flavor that best describes Mars. But I can also feel Caleb thinking. "I said shut up," I repeat.

"I didn't say anything," he huffs.

"You're distracting me."

"Distracting you from what?"

"From using my super power," I reply.

"Oh, fuck me in half," Caleb mutters, dragging a hand through his hair and leaning up against the glass door of the Talenti gelatos. "Seriously with this? It's not a super power, Jake. It's not anything."

I shoot daggers at him with my eyes. "You're just jealous."

He scoffs. "Why would I be jealous?"

"Because it means I can read people better than you," I reply.

"You think I need to know Mars' favorite ice cream flavor to know him?"

"It helps," I say with a shrug.

Cay snorts. "Go on then, Superman. Walk me through it. What ice cream flavor is he?"

I narrow my eyes back at the wall of glass. "I've already ruled out cookies, caramel, anything with fruit, and anything special edition. Mars is the old reliable type. He wants something he can count on. He likes routine. I bet he treats eating dessert like he treats a cheat meal. It's a mild indulgence for him."

"So, nothing flashy?" Caleb says. I know the asshole is curious. He's glancing at the case. I see his wheels turning too. "Maybe he's a plain vanilla guy."

I snort. "There's nothing vanilla about him. No, he's suave and sophisticated and European. He's got that awesome full back tattoo, meaning he's got an artsy side. Even if he can't do art, he can appreciate it. And he listens to that crazy death metal music all the time. No, he's not a vanilla. Or a plain chocolate."

Now Caleb is looking earnestly at the case, his annoyance forgotten. "Coffee?"

"No. He drinks coffee, he doesn't eat it. I'm thinking something with nuts," I explain. Actually, it's helping to talk it out. "But he's definitely not a Butter Pecan guy. That's too American."

"How do you know he's a Häagen-Dazs flavor?" Caleb teases.

He laughs, but it's a serious question. I shake my head with a sigh. "I don't. That's the problem." But now I'm invested. I want to get this right. I want to show Mars how well I can read him. And fine, I wanna show Caleb too. "He might just be the toughest nut I've tried to crack," I admit.

"Oh, so you're tryin' to crack his nuts? Something you're not telling me, Superman?" There's a laugh in his tone, but his eyes are serious. Caleb is territorial. Whatever we are— me and him; me and Rachel; me, him, and Rachel—it's enough to have him on edge.

"No," I reply, gently. "I'm not interested in Mars as anything other than a friend...and the occasional fuck buddy. You gotta admit, he's impressive. I bet he's riding Rachel ragged with that monster co—"

"Shut up," Caleb growls, pushing off the cooler to shove my arm.

"What's the matter? You jealous? This whole sharing thing not working for you? I'll happily accept your defeat. Just means more Rachel for me—"

"I'm not jealous," he mutters, lowering his voice as an old lady comes around the corner pushing a full shopping cart. "I'm just free-ballin' it in these shorts," he adds, discreetly adjusting himself.

I snort, my nose catching a whiff of his crisp cologne as he steps in closer, letting the lady pass behind us. I stifle a groan. I hate how much I react to even just the smell of his cologne. My skin feels like it's tingling and I wanna bury my face at his neck and breathe him in.

And I don't know if it was intentional, but as he shifts, his crotch brushes against the outside of my hand.

Holy fuck.

He's getting hard right here in the ice cream aisle. Thinking about Rachel with Mars is turning him on. Fuck, now *I'm* getting turned on thinking about *him* being turned on.

"Will you just pick one?" he mutters.

6

I blink, refocusing on the wall of ice creams. "I've narrowed it down to two," I say. "He's either a Pistachio, or a Vanilla Swiss Almond."

"I thought we said no vanilla?" he replies crossing his arms over his chest. "Come on, it's freezing. Pick already."

I slow turn toward him with a frown. "We live on an ice rink and you're cold? Really?"

"It's the juxtaposition," he replies in that authoritative, I-was-a-chemistry-major tone he gets sometimes. "The warm air behind us is mixing with the cold and it's giving me the chills. Just pick a damn ice cream, so we can go."

"Fine," I huff, swinging open the freezer door. "Pistachio it is." I snatch up a pint and toss it into the basket, letting the door whisper shut.

"So, why Pistachio?" Caleb says, leading the way towards the cash register.

"Because Mars is a health nut and pistachios are supposed to be, like, really healthy, right?"

"I guess," Caleb says with a shrug.

"Plus Pistachio just seems to fit his whole vibe," I add.

"His vibe?"

"Yeah, you know his whole moody, broody, silently thoughtful thing. Like he never says a word, right? But he's always there, and he's always paying attention. He sees *everything*. And he just seems to like *know* things, you know? That feels more like a Pistachio than a Vanilla Swiss Almond."

"Whatever you say," he says with a laugh.

I frown. "You still don't believe this is a super power."

"Of course I don't."

I shove the basket at him, crossing my arms. "Okay, then allow me to go on—"

"I really wish you wouldn't—"

7

"Some flavors insist on themselves," I say. "Like Birthday Cake. Seriously? What's wrong with just eating cake? Why do I need an ice cream that tastes like cake? With Mars, what you see is exactly what you get. He's not a liar, posing as one thing when he's really another. And he doesn't change on you either, like a fancy special edition flavor, here one month, gone the next. Mars is always in the crease, doing his job. Whether you see him or not, whether he's the focus of attention or not, he's standing in front of that goal. Same with Pistachio. It's always there. People may overlook it, thinking it's a funky flavor or even a boring flavor, but it's not. It's reassuring and delicious."

Caleb frowns. "So Mars is Pistachio ice cream to you? Reassuring, always there, silent, and real...and delicious, apparently?"

I nod, liking his list. "Yep. Plus, you know, it seemed the most European," I add. "I could imagine him on vacation in Italy with some hot Finnish girl, walking by the Trevi Fountain, sharing a scoop of pistachio gelato."

Caleb snorts, handing the basket over to the cashier.. "He's with a hot Finnish girl, huh?"

"Well, I mean, now all I can see is Mars with Rachel. He looks at her like *she's* ice cream. Know what I mean?"

He makes some noncommittal response before ducking down and snatching up a pack of cinnamon gum. He adds it to the pile of ice creams.

"You think he loves her?" I ask, arms crossed as I watch the cashier swipe all our ice creams across the scanner. Mine goes first, then Caleb's, then Rachel's, then the new pint of Pistachio. It feels symbolic somehow. Four ice creams, four different flavors, but ultimately all the same.

Caleb stands right next to me. When he crosses his

arms, our elbows brush. Just when I think he's not going to reply, he does. "Yeah, I do," he says, his tone solemn.

"You think he can ever learn to love us too?" I ask, not daring to look his way. "And not in the gay way—I mean, I know he doesn't—not like that," I reply, tugging my wallet from my pocket. "I wasn't implying—"

"I know what you meant," he replies.

I work my card through the machine, typing in my pin. "Well?" I repeat. "Do you?"

As I tuck my card back inside my wallet he sighs, shaking his head. "We'll have to see. Let's just hope you didn't fuck this all up and get him Pistachio ice cream when he's allergic to nuts. Hurricane'll never forgive you if you poison him to death."

"Wait—is he allergic to nuts?" I say, suddenly anxious that he might be right. Come to think of it, I don't think I've ever seen Mars eat a nut.

Oh shit...

Caleb ignores me, thanking the cashier and snatching up our bags.

"Cay, is he allergic to nuts?" I say again, taking the receipt from the cashier.

But he's already on the move, walking with a hitch in his step towards the sliding glass doors.

"Cay!" I shout.

He doesn't turn around.

"Fucking hell," I mutter, tossing the receipt into the trash. I call a frazzled 'thanks' to the cashier and hurry after him. I either got this right on the money...or I'm about to send my girlfriend's boyfriend into anaphylactic shock. Hey, at least she's a doctor, right?

This is all gonna be fine.

"Cay, wait up!"

2

EMERGENCY CONTACT

RACHEL

I s there anything better than ending a glorious day off with your feet up on the coffee table, a trashy movie on Netflix, and a pint of ice cream in hand? I dig in with my spoon, savoring the tart taste of my mango sorbet.

I'm only half-watching this romcom. It's hard to concentrate when my phone is dinging every two minutes with updates from Harrison. Their surrogate is currently in labor and my twin has zero freaking chill. I'm trying to be the supportive sister-slash-godmother, but there's only so many times in so many ways that I can tell him contractions are perfectly normal before I'm gonna have to just mute my phone.

My bags are already packed and perched by the door because my guys and I leave in the morning for Seattle. We're all going out to see the new baby. The timing is perfect, really. We have to be back in four days for the start of training camp and then it will be impossible to get away.

Not that Davita planned her labor to fit our work schedules...

The low electric hum of the garage alerts me to my guys

being back. They all played a pickup game of hockey over at the practice rink tonight, and then went out to dinner with the team. Karaoke night at Rip's is a weekly favorite, but I was just too in love with the idea of no bra and the house to myself to bother joining in the fun tonight. They're bringing me a doggy bag of chicken wings and waffle fries.

Which probably means I should lose the sorbet, right? I look down at the melty orange dessert with a wistful sigh.

Hopping of the couch, I pad silently over to the kitchen in my socks and put the lid back on the sorbet. Slipping it back into the freezer, I glance over my shoulder at the wall of sliding glass and smirk at my reflection. I look like a hot mess—hair up in a tangled knot, smudged makeup. I'm wearing my rattiest cropped Ferrymen sweatshirt that hangs off one shoulder, and a pair of hot pink granny panties.

I quickly toss my used spoon in the dishwasher, eager to hide any proof of eating my dessert before dinner...a dinner of greasy, fried hot wings and over salted potato fries. Yeah, my diet has been all over the place. I've been having the weirdest cravings. But it's my day off, and I'm living it up right with popcorn, sorbet, and hot wings. And I'm gonna eat it all in my underwear. What can I say? If my guys can't love trash panda Rachel, they certainly don't deserve smoke show Rachel.

I hear the metallic whine of the garage door coming back down. Sy is already dancing by the door, eager to see his daddies.

I open the fridge, bending over to peer down low, looking for a sparkling water.

"God, you are being *so* overdramatic right now," comes Jake's heated voice.

"Oh, that's rich coming from you," Caleb replies.

I jerk upright, bottle of San Pellegrino in hand, and close the fridge.

My guys come marching through the kitchen, Jake in the lead.

"Stop fighting," says Ilmari from just behind him. "It's not important."

"Wait, you did *not* just say that," Jake cries, wholly incredulous as he spins around to glare at Ilmari. "It's not *important*? I'm sorry, but do you want me to punch you or pack your fucking bags?"

Ilmari sighs. "I didn't mean it like that."

Jake crosses his arms and glares. "Well, what *did* you mean?"

Caleb is the last in from the garage, Poseidon skirting around his legs, oblivious to their obvious tension. Caleb steps around Ilmari's broad frame, his dark eyes locking on me as he holds out a white paper takeout bag stamped with the Rip's logo.

"What's wrong?" I say, glancing between them as I take the bag.

"Apparently, Mars here is Jake's best friend," Caleb replies, jerking his thumb over his shoulder at Ilmari. "He only announced it to the whole fucking team right in front of me as if I didn't exist."

I blink, glancing between them. "Wait—what happened?"

Jake turns to face me. "Novy was annoyed that I was sharing my fries with Mars because I never let him share my food. But okay, A—" He holds a finger up in the air. "Novy is a fucking pig, and when you give him an inch, he takes a mile. I share my fries, I have no fucking fries. And B—" He holds up a second finger. "Mars is my best fucking friend. You share your fries with your best friend. It's like a rule, right? And I said all this to Novy, but Cay overheard me, and now he's acting all butt hurt like he's not my fucking husband."

"I just wanna know the difference," Caleb replies, turning away from me to cross his arms and glare at Jake. "I thought I was your best friend—"

"You're my husband," Jake shouts. "Fuck, is saying it in English not working? Tú eres mi esposo, loco."

"Oh, don't go showing off your Spanish," Caleb growls.

Behind Jake, Ilmari raises a blond brow. "You speak Spanish?"

Ilmari and I share a glance. Color me curious too.

"I have a whole fucking college degree in Spanish," Jake replies with a wave of his hand, not turning around.

Somehow, this doesn't compute for me. "Wait—your major was Spanish?"

"Yes," he and Caleb say at the same time.

"How did I not know this?" I say, pursing my lips. Has it really never come up in over a year of marriage?

"He only picked it because the Spanish Club brought food to all their events," Caleb replies with a scoff.

"Hey, if you'd ever tried Profesora Ortega's homemade empanadas, you would have majored in Spanish too," Jake snaps, pointing a finger in Caleb's face. "But don't change the fucking subject. Are you seriously mad that I said Mars is my best friend? Cause we need to get that out in the open. Communication, right? Kitchen rules apply. Sudden death."

"I'm not playing sudden death with you right now," Caleb huffs.

"Mars *is* my best friend," Jake all but shouts. "God, what have we been building towards for the last two years if not this?" he adds, gesturing around at the four of us. "He's my best friend now. We live together, we work together, we fuck

13

our wife together. I fold his damn underwear. Hell, we go on sunset beach walks together. But you're my *husband*, Cay."

Caleb glare at him. "Yeah? And what does that get me?"

Jake just blinks at him, mouth open on a pant. "Well... how about some pretty fucking amazing sex, for one? When you're not being a total fucking asshole," he adds. "Mars is the guy I share my fries with. You're the guy I share my *soul* with."

Caleb crosses his arms and glares. "What does that mean to you?"

Jake glances from Ilmari to me, clearly looking for some help. But I feel like it's important that I don't interfere.

"Well—I—you have to be my emergency contact," Jake says.

Caleb narrows his eyes. "Your emergency contact?"

"Yeah, you know, like if I get hit by a bus or injured on the ice," Jake says with a wave of his hand. "You have to pick up the phone and take that call."

Caleb rolls his eyes. "So that's it for you then? The difference between me and Mars is that I get to fuck you and I have to claim your remains when you get steamrolled by a bus?"

"Can we please stop talking about Jake dying in a tragic bus accident?" I say.

He and Jake look my way and then Caleb is pointing at me. "What about her? What is she to you?"

Jake's jaw clenches tight in anger. "She's my wife, asshole. Keep pointing at her like that, and I'll break your fucking finger off."

"So why isn't she your emergency contact?" he presses. "Why me?"

"Because you're my husband!" Jake bellows. "Fuck, am I gonna have to tattoo it on your forehead? Rachel is my wife.

14

She's my whole fucking world. But we're *legally* married, Cay. That means *you* have to be my emergency contact. It's like, the law...right?" He glances at me, desperately looking for validation.

I bite my lip, really unsure if I should interfere. But now they're all looking at me. "Umm...well, technically you can put anyone you want as your emergency contact," I reply.

Some of Jake's anger dissipates. "Wait, seriously?"

"Yeah, it's just whoever you want contacted first in case of an emergency," Caleb replies.

Jake's shoulders slump a little. "I thought it had to be like your partner or a legal family member."

"When I first joined the Rays, Coach Tomlin was my emergency contact," Ilmari says with a shrug. "I didn't know anyone else."

"Wait," I say, holding up a hand, glaring at Jake. "You put Caleb as your emergency contact? Why would you do that when I'm a literal doctor?"

Jake looks like a vein is about to pop in his temple. "Because Caleb is my fucking husband!"

"Wait—" says Caleb. "Mars, you've updated your paperwork though, right? Did you put Rachel down as your emergency contact?"

We all turn to look at our broody Finn. He's standing by the range, arms crossed in his Rays tech shirt. He glances from Caleb to me, his blue eyes giving nothing away.

"Oh shit," Jake says on a breath. "He didn't. Mars, you didn't write down your own wife as your emergency contact?"

"No," he replies softly, looking at me.

Damn, why is this actually hurting my feelings right now? This is silly, right? This whole argument is ridiculous. We must be uncovering something deeper.

"Why?" I murmur, setting my unopened water on the island. "Why wouldn't you pick me? I'm a doctor, Ilmari."

"Yes, but in the moment of my injury, you wouldn't be my doctor," he reasons. "You would be my wife, Rakas. And I would spare you any pain."

His gentle words have tears springing to my eyes. "Ilmari—"

"I would want any news of my injury to be mediated for you through the careful attention of one who loves you."

"Which of us did you pick?" Caleb asks.

Ilmari holds his gaze.

Caleb's eyes go wide as Jake huffs an incredulous laugh.

"Great, so we both picked Caleb," Jake says with a wave of his hand. "So in the event of my best friend getting hit by a bus, I'll have to hear about it from Rachel who will wait to hear about it from Cay. That's just great. I'll be the last to know you could be in mortal peril. Feels really fucking good. Maybe I'll rescind your best friend badge and give it to Poseidon."

The dog barks at hearing his name, nudging Jake's hand.

"Wait," says Ilmari with a raised hand of his own. He focuses his full attention on me. "Rakas, who did you pick?"

I glance between my guys. *Shit.* "Umm…"

"Oh, don't you even fucking say it," Jake groans. "You picked Cay too, didn't you?"

I bite my lip, looking to Ilmari. God damn it, I hate to see that look in his eyes. It doesn't really matter, right?

"I'm your husband, Rakas," he says, the hurt evident in his tone.

"Yes, and I love you more than my own life," I reply, stepping closer. "And you're usually the most even-tempered man I know. But, love, you *do* have a tendency to go a little crazy where I'm concerned."

He growls his annoyance. "Nonsense."

This earns a snort from Jake and an eye roll from Caleb.

"Okay...well, what happened the last time we all went out to dinner?" I challenge.

"We had sushi," he replies tonelessly.

"Yes, and what did you do when my order came out wrong?"

He glares at me. "I don't see how getting a waitress to correct your order counts as going crazy."

Jake scoffs again. "You made that waitress cry, Mars. I had to tip her forty percent so I could show my face in there again."

Ilmari just keep his big arms folded over his chest, saying nothing.

"And what about our last game of beach volleyball?" I press. "Langley spiked the ball and I dove to get it and landed funny on my knee and what did you do?"

"This is ridiculous," he mutters.

"You carried me *three* blocks back to the house to clean out the scrapes and get me an ice pack," I say for him. "You wouldn't let me walk, even after I said I was fine. You really think I want you being the one making major medical decisions on my behalf?"

"I'm your husband," he growls.

"Hurts, doesn't it?" Jake jabs.

I spin to face Caleb. "Well, wait a second. All three of us put *you* down as our emergency contact. Who did you write? You can't write yourself."

"He wrote you, of course," says Jake. "Just promise me you'll send me a postcard from the hospital, yeah?"

But I hold Caleb's gaze, watching the way his jaw clenches.

"He didn't," says Ilmari. "He didn't write Rachel either."

Caleb groans, dragging a hand through his messy beach curls.

"Wait—you didn't write Rachel?" says Jake, his tone brightening. "Oh my god, babe, did you write me? I'm your emergency contact?"

Caleb pulls his apologetic gaze from me, turning to Jake. He takes a step forward, reaching out a hand. "Babe, listen—"

"Oh, fuck no." Jake jerks away. "Do *not* tell me you picked Mars. I swear to fucking god, Cay."

Caleb closes the space between them, grabbing Jake by the upper arm. "Jake, I love you—"

"Spare me," he huffs, trying to pull away, but Caleb grips him by the other arm and steps in.

"I love you, and I love Rachel—"

"Clearly," Jake scoffs.

"But if I'm lying in a hospital bed, I'm sorry, but I want Mars to be the one with the power to unplug me," he goes on.

"Wait, so in this situation I'm ending your life?" Ilmari says with a horrified look on his face.

"Hey, it could happen," Caleb replies with a shrug. "You're the only one who will consider rationally and weigh all the evidence. These two will just demand they do everything to keep my heart beating. You'll know when it's time to let me go."

"Jeeeezus," Jake says, his face suddenly ashen. "Do you have to be so morbid about it?"

"I hate talking about bus crashes and death beds," I echo. "It's really freaking me out, and I was having a great day up until now."

"So I'm no one's emergency contact," Jake huffs, flapping his arms. "In case of emergency, when one of the three loves of my fucking life may be in actual mortal peril, I'll have as much right to get a phone call as Poseidon?"

Hearing his name, the dog barks again.

"I cannot believe that I'm a *literal* fucking doctor, and yet not a single one of you put me down as your emergency contact," I say.

"Guys, this isn't a big deal," Caleb reasons. "It's just a name on a form—"

"Easy for you to say," Jake snaps, trying to jerk away again. "It's *your* name on all the fucking forms."

Caleb's dark eyes narrow on Jake, his shoulders going tense. "You know, I'm getting really fucking sick of your attitude. Mouth off me to me again, and I'll show that mouth what it's good for."

Jake's eyes go wide, anger and resentment etched on every line of his face. "Don't you *dare* try to turn me on right now. I'm really upset about this, asshole. You know how much I need to feel needed. This really hurts that none of you put my name down."

"Jake," I say gently, inching closer. "We love you. We don't want to hurt you. We would never want to put you in that awful position of hearing the news first, of making you have to be the one to tell the others. We were protecting you."

"Well it feels a lot like getting shoved to the side. Last fucking place," he mutters.

I place my hand on his arm just above Caleb's. "First place," I say. "Jake, we love you. And this is nothing," I say with a wave of my hand. "Details. As mundane as a grocery list. We had paperwork, we filled it out. But we all know the reality here," I add, glancing around at all three of them. "One team, right? One family. Four strong. It doesn't matter who hears first that Caleb was attacked by a jellyfish at the beach. We're all in this together. Forget husbands and wives and legal or illegal. The labels don't matter. At least, they don't to me. Be my best friend, be my husband, my lover, my partner. Pick any label you want, just be *mine*."

This seems to ease Jake a bit, he relaxes slightly, giving me a little nod.

"You're mine," Caleb echoes, voice firm as he leans in to brush his lips at the corner of Jake's mouth. "You're fucking mine." He sinks against Jake, pinning him to the counter with his hips, their foreheads touching.

Jake's hands lift, bracing Cay at the elbows.

"You're mine," Caleb repeats, one hand raising to cup Jake's stubbled cheek.

"Show me," Jake replies, his resentment giving way to heat and raw need. He drops a hand down between them, cupping Caleb's dick through his shorts. "Show me all the ways I'm yours—"

He barely gets the words out before Cay is kissing him. They moan against each other's mouths, opening deep, their hands setting blazing paths as they touch all the skin they can reach, lighting each other up.

I hold back a whimper, my core going from ice floe to volcano.

"Oh fuck," Jake pants, breaking their kiss. His head tips back, eyes closed, as Caleb drops his mouth down to suck on his neck, one hand slipping inside Jake's athletic shorts. "Fuck me," Jake begs. "Cay, please—"

Caleb silences him with another kiss, but it doesn't last long before he's pulling back, panting for breath. "Mars, get the fuck over here."

Ilmari steps closer. I watch, heart in my throat, as he inches into their space.

"Anything to say to our guy?" Caleb says, his heated gaze still locked on Jake.

Ilmari's large hand grabs Jake roughly by the jaw, turning him. Then he's leaning in, his blue eyes like fiery ice. "You're mine," he growls. Surprising the fuck out of all of us, he presses his lips to Jake's mouth, kissing him.

Caleb leans away, eyes wide, as Ilmari teases his tongue into Jake's mouth. Jake moans, kissing him back, chasing his touch. My whole body hums as I try to keep the pieces of myself from shattering. Then Ilmari breaks his kiss with Jake, his hand already cupping the back of Caleb's neck. Cay has no time to pull away before Ilmari is kissing him too.

"Oh fuck," Jake whines, his gaze molten as he watches them.

Caleb more than reciprocates, one hand leaving Jake's side to take hold of Ilmari.

Ilmari breaks the kiss and all three of them are panting. "You're both mine," he says. "Fight over me again, and I'll tape your dicks together."

Jake huffs a laugh as Caleb glares at him.

"Now fuck each other while I fuck our wife," he says, shoving away from them as he steps around Cay's back, his eyes locked on me.

I hold back a whimper as he crashes into me. Both arms band around me as he pulls me close, silencing my breathless cry with his mouth. We kiss like we're starving for it. Knowing his lips are warm from kissing our guys has me melting. His sexual preferences are completely his own choice, but I can't deny how it makes me ravenous to see my guys all love each other. He initiated it. He *wanted* it. He wanted to connect with them in that way and I am here for it one thousand fucking percent.

He spins me around, jerking my panties down, as he lifts

me up, plopping my bare ass down on the kitchen island. I hiss at the cold feel of the granite on my cheeks, at such odds with the fire burning in my blood. Spreading my legs, he drops to his knees, covering my needy pussy with his mouth.

"Oh—" I cry, arching back as I fist his hair. I fling my other hand back, bracing against the counter.

He slips my legs over his shoulders, squeezing me tight around his face as he devours me, licking and sucking my clit.

"God—fuck—" I whine, my orgasm already spiraling so tight. "Don't stop. Kulta, please—"

He pulls my thighs apart, spreading me wide as he shoves two thick fingers up inside me. Tongue teasing my clit, he works his fingers in like a jackhammer, power fucking me.

"Fuck," I scream, head tipped back as I press past that feeling of needing to pee. "Ohmygod, ohmygod," I cry, toes curling tight, legs cramping. My whole body unravels as I squirt, my pussy leaking into his mouth, gushing like a fountain.

Between my legs, Ilmari groans like a feral beast, swallowing every drop.

I'm wrung out, boneless. Squirting is so rare for me. It's only happened two other times. Both with him. I don't know what pussy magic he possesses, but he's officially the king of eating me out.

Next to us, Caleb is on his knees, sucking Jake's cock with hot, slurping sounds.

"Oh my fucking god," Jake groans, head tipped back, both hands fisting Caleb's hair. "More. Need more."

Caleb pops off him, getting to his feet. He looks to me

and I nod. I need more too. I need them all. This moment feels too important to play on tag teams.

"You call the shots, babe," he says at me.

I nod again, tapping Ilmari's shoulder. He rocks back on his heels and I slip off the counter to the floor. I'm still wearing my Ferrymen sweatshirt. I jerk it off and toss it, leaving me naked. Why do I always end up naked in this kitchen?

"I want you all," I say. "Now. Caleb in my pussy, Jake in my ass. Ilmari, baby, fuck my face."

Ilmari stands and Caleb leans in, wrapping a hand around my neck to pull me in for a kiss. He breaks it quick and nods. "Mars, living room. Move the table. Jake, get the lube."

He drops his hand away from me and my guys split in three different directions. I watch from the kitchen as Caleb calls to the dog, putting him outside. Ilmari makes quick work of moving the coffee table, tossing a few blankets and pillows down onto the carpeted floor.

Jake reappears in moments, bottle of lube in hand. "Seattle, let's go," he calls. "Bring me that sweet fucking ass."

I smile, my heart feeling so full as I watch my three guys come together in our living room, dropping their clothes to the floor. There's no shame, no awkwardness. They're all in. I walk around the end of the island, feeling like a queen, the endorphins of one orgasm already humming through my veins.

Caleb walks over to the wall, adjusting the lights on the wall panel, bringing down the brightness to set a more intimate mood. Ilmari uses the remote to turn on the electric fireplace. He knows how much I like stretching out naked in front of it, my post-sex glow warm on my skin. Meanwhile, Jake is already on his knees, fixing the blankets.

They know me. They take such good care of me. Who cares that I'm not their emergency contact? I'm the center of their collective universe.

With a smile, I flamingo each leg, tugging off my fuzzy socks. Nothing kills the mood for me quite like socks on feet during sex. My smile widens, seeing that all my guys have already done the same.

Ilmari is standing closest, his hand casually pumping his hard cock. He watches me with a heated gaze. "Come, Rakas."

I step forward, my hand wrapping around his on his dick as I tip up on my toes, kissing him again. He tastes like me and I fucking love it.

Caleb steps in behind me, his hard cock pressing at my ass, his hands slipping between me and Ilmari to cup my breasts. His warm mouth settles on my neck, kissing up my ear then down my shoulder. He tweaks my nipples as Ilmari drops his mouth down to kiss the other side of my neck. I sigh, head tipping back, luxuriating in the feel of them.

Jake steps in and his hand smooths over my hip, down to cup my pussy. He groans, his fingers slipping through my wetness, circling my tender clit as I hum with need. I bite my lip, sinking into this perfect feeling of being touched by all three of them at once.

Jake's fingers sink in deep. "Kiss me," he says.

Caleb pulls back, making room for him so we can kiss. I love the taste of my Jake, the feel of his soft lips. He's always the most groomed in the facial hair department. His upper lip is baby smooth as we open and tease, tongues flicking.

Then Caleb's hand is at Jake's neck, pulling him back to take his turn. I'm right there, sharing breath with them as they kiss, my hand still stroking Ilmari's cock. Jake pulls away on a pant, his eyes glassy with need as he drops his face forward, kissing Ilmari's shoulder and up his neck.

Ilmari groans, letting him do it as he finds my mouth, claiming me with the strength of his kiss.

Caleb steps to my side, his hand reaching up to grab Ilmari's top knot, fisting tight. He lowers his mouth too, kissing the other side of his neck.

"No niin," Ilmari groans, eyes shut tight as Jake and Caleb suck the sides of his neck.

I'm weak with need watching them. Fierce love boils up inside of me, threatening to burn me to ash. They're mine. My loves. My family. I will protect them from any danger, run through fire for them, burn the world for them.

Jake and Caleb pull away, both breathless, chests heaving. It's Caleb who speaks, still gripping tight to Ilmari's top knot. "You're fucking ours," he says, intensity lacing his tone. "You're not our friend. You're *ours*."

Ilmari nods, swallowing down whatever emotions he's feeling. "Yours." Then he glances down at me, need burning in his eyes. "Yours," he says again, his gaze locked on me.

"Mine," I echo. "Forever. No way out."

"No way out," he repeats, lowering his face to kiss me.

Jake moves his fingers inside me again, working my clit with his thumb. He sinks a third finger inside, stretching me out. "Baby, can I take you with Mars?" he asks, peppering kisses on my shoulder. "Please," he begs. He looks to Ilmari. "Will you do DVP with me? Is that like, a limit for you or..."

I hold my breath, waiting for Ilmari to speak. He shares me with them all the time. Double penetration is nothing new. I know Caleb is his secret favorite. My not-so-straight husband loves himself a little ribbed cock action.

But he's never been in my pussy with one of them

before. Cocks pressed together as my walls hold them tight...

Oh god, I'm ready to explode just thinking about it.

Ilmari looks to me, a question in his eyes. "I don't want to hurt you," he murmurs. "My size—"

I silence him with a kiss, knowing he's in. "You won't," I say through breathless kisses. "Kulta, you won't. Let Jake show you how. Please, baby, I need you both so badly." I hold to his shoulders, clinging to him, pouring out my aching need.

"We'll make it so good for you," Jake says at me, kissing me again as Ilmari pulls away.

Caleb has already dropped to one knee, rearranging a few pillows against the couch. "Mars, lie down," he directs. "Jake needs to run this show. Your fat cock will stretch her out, and we'll help you get her ready."

Ilmari drops to his knees, pulling me down with him. I kiss across his chest, my hands slipping around to fist his firm ass. His hands do the same, pulling me to him. He tips my mouth up with a hand under my chin, claiming my lips.

Caleb drops down behind us, his hands smoothing over my hips and down to cup my pussy. I press back against his hips, widening my stance on my knees so he can slip three fingers in. I moan, biting Ilmari's bottom lip, loving the feeling of Caleb's fingers pumping deep.

"You're such a good fucking girl," Caleb murmurs behind me. If Ilmari gets first prize in eating me out, Caleb is the king of dirty talk. This man can talk me to orgasm. And he has. More than once. Including once at a hospital fundraiser dinner. I swear to god, Poppy was sitting across the table from us and I think she knew what was up because ever since, she doesn't put Caleb and I at the same table.

Fucking worth it.

"You want to take two cocks at once, baby," he teases. "Want Jake and Mars to fill this perfect fucking pussy?"

"Yes," I whimper.

"Want them to fill you so fucking tight?"

"Yes—"

"They're going to make a mess of you. Our perfect good whore, so desperate for our cum. You'll take it all, won't you?"

"Yes—*ah*—" I gasp, my body shuddering as he slips his fingers out and slaps my pussy.

"God, I love your dirty fucking mouth," Jake growls, pulling back on Cay and stealing his air with a filthy kiss. It's hot and messy and they both moan into it.

"Turn around," Ilmari orders. "Watch them while I stretch you."

He helps me turn, one hand at my hip and one gripping tight to my shoulder, as he bends me forward and down, notching his cock between my legs.

"Take me," he says. "All the way."

On a breathless moan, I sink back onto him, my body adjusting to that first exquisite, painful stretch. It zings straight through me, crackling in my chest, down my finger-tips. And then he's moving, thrusting himself deeper.

Kneeling before me, Caleb has his cock fisted tight with Jake's. At some point lube was added, making his hand slick and shiny. They both groan as Caleb works them both over, pulling with slow, luxurious strokes. No one is in a hurry. We all want this moment to last.

"Look at you riding that big cock," Caleb teases, turning to watch as Ilmari sinks himself all the way in. "How does she feel, Mars?"

"Incredible," he replies.

I bask in their praise as he rocks deep inside me. Then I

cry out, my eyes opening wide with surprise as the sound of Ilmari's slap reaches my ears. My ass cheek stings, the sharp heat burning through my skin and making my clit pulse. "Do it again," I say, slamming his hips with mine. "Harder."

Ilmari lifts both hands from my hips and slaps either sides of my ass with a grunt.

"Oh fuck," I whine, my head drooping between my shoulders as I give over to the sensation.

Caleb's fist on my hair has me looking up at him, head tipped back. "Open," he growls, his dick tapping my lips.

I open for him, teasing his tip before I suck, his piercings gliding over my tongue. I don't even mind the strawberry flavored lube.

He keeps his fist tight in my hair. "Again," he orders, moving his hips to press deeper inside my mouth. "Harder."

Ilmari's large palm all but covers my ass as he slaps me hard, the sting making me squeeze his cock so tight he groans. With Caleb all but choking me on his cock, I'm ready to see stars. My orgasm coils high and tight.

Caleb lets me go and I suck in air, saliva dripping down my chin. "Oh god," I whine. "Please, please, more—*ah*—"

Caleb takes me by the throat, lifting me up off all fours so I'm on my knees, Ilmari rocking deep behind me. He lifts me by my hips, all but placing me in his lap as he buries himself inside me. Caleb inches closer, his hand holding firm pressure at my throat.

"Our good fucking girl likes it rough," he says, his dark eyes molten with hunger. "She likes to be owned and fucked. Used. Don't you?"

I nod, a tear slipping down my cheek as he chokes me, his pressure steady and even. I reach up, my hand wrapping around his wrist, ready to tell him if I've had enough.

With one hand at my throat, he drops his other between my legs. "Mars, hold on. Hold still."

Ilmari holds me still, his warm breath fanning over my shoulder.

Caleb relaxes his hand at my throat as he uses his other to press two fingers in with Ilmari's cock.

"Fuck," Ilmari pants. "Caleb—"

"You like that?" Caleb teases. "Like that stretch? Just wait till Jake is pounding you both. You better cum all over his dick, Mars. And when you're done, I'm licking you clean. No other man wears my husband's cum unless I get a taste. That's the rule. Agreed?"

Ilmari is silent behind me, but I feel him nod.

"Good," says Cay, a triumphant smile on his face. "Then lie down. We're doing this."

Ilmari slips out of me and I sort of fall forward into Caleb's embrace. My body hums with the need to come again. I watch as Ilmari lies down in a half recline, his back supported against the couch by the pillows. His proud cock rests hard and ready between his legs.

"Ride him, Hurricane," Caleb directs. "Face him."

I nod, dropping down to crawl over to Ilmari. He helps me shift over his lap, his strong hands at my hips. I nestle my pussy at the base of his dick, tipping up onto my knees. "You ready?"

He nods back, giving my hips a squeeze.

I sink down on him, adjusting my hips, taking him deep until he fills me so full.

"Spread your legs, Mars," Jake says from behind me. As Ilmari shifts, Jake drops to his knees. His firm hands work their way up my back to my shoulders. "Bend over, baby girl. That's it. So fucking perfect."

29

Ilmari helps me curl forward, supporting some of my weight, as Jake smooths his hands over my ass.

"Gonna use my fingers first," says Jake.

Ilmari and I both hold our breath, gazing into each other's eyes as we feel Jake's fingers press in. I bite my bottom lip, eyes falling shut as Jake curls his fingers along my inner wall, stretching me out.

"God, I need in this pussy," Jake groans. "Wanna feel you both. Mars, just tell me to stop and it stops—"

"Do it," Ilmari grunts beneath me. "Take us."

I brace my hands against Ilmari's chest, taking several short, shallow breaths as Jake presses in behind me, the tip of his lubed dick brushing feather light against my skin.

"Breathe for me, baby," Jake soothes.

I suck in a breath, pushing it out as he presses in with the tip of his dick, stretching me, helping me open.

"Oh god," I whimper. "Oh fuck. Do it. Fuck me, angel. Get inside."

The stretch is intense. Ilmari is already so large all on his own, and Jake is big too. My men whisper soft words of encouragement in English and Finnish as Jake works himself in, filling me so full.

Tears sting the corners of my eyes as I breathe through the sensation of my men sharing me in this way for the first time.

"You are well?" Ilmari murmurs, raising a hand to brush my tear away.

I nod, desperate for more. "Yes. Jake, baby, please. Fuck me, please. Fuck us."

Jake's hands smooth over my ass to grip my hips. "Hold on tight, Seattle."

I suck in a breath and then he pulls out to just the tip, slamming back in.

"Fuck," I cry. "Oh, god—"

"Helvetti," Ilmari groans, his hands at my sides, helping to support my weight.

"How does it feel?" Jake says, his hands smoothing up and down my hips as he rocks into me, into us.

"So fucking good," I whimper. "Jake—fuck—"

He laughs, moving his hips, his cock sliding tight against Ilmari as he moves in and out of my aching, needy pussy.

Ilmari groans, head tipped back, eyes shut tight. It's all he can do to hold off his orgasm as he fights the feeling of Jake's silky smooth cock railing us both hard.

"Cay," I cry out, nearly delirious with the rapid fire sensations sparking through my body. "Cay—I need—"

I can't even finish the sentence. The sentiment is there. *Need.* I need all three of them. My men. My loves. Mine.

"Up," he orders, pulling on my shoulder.

Ilmari keeps supporting me, my hands pressed on his chest, as Caleb pulls me up one handed, his other wrapped around the base of his cock.

I sink my mouth around him, knowing all three of my men are filling me, and my orgasm bursts like a super nova. My legs shake and my breathing stutters as my release hits me in waves. I'm exploding outward, even as my pussy tries to pull everything in. I squeeze them so tight both Jake and Ilmari curse and groan.

Jake's movement hitches. "I can't—*fuck*—ahh, god—" He loses control, coming inside me all over Ilmari's dick.

Meanwhile, I make a mess of sucking Caleb's cock as I pant and mewl like a helpless creature, spit on my chin as I suck his tip. He works his base, his other hand gripping tight to my hair.

Beneath me, Ilmari slams up with his hips, sending both Jake and I spiraling. He grunts, chasing his release. Mine is still fluttering, the final cascades not yet over, as I moan around Caleb's cock, tasting him on my tongue.

"I'm coming," Ilmari groans.

"Oh god—" Jake slumps over my back, his hard cock pulsing with Ilmari's inside me as they both fill me so full.

"Fuck—take it," Caleb groans next to me. "My good fucking girl. Take it all."

He slaps his dick against my tongue as he jerks his own shaft. I take it like a greedy whore, letting him come in my open mouth. A whiny sound escapes my lips as I gaze up at him, loving the heat in his eyes as he stares right back at me, watching as his cum paints my lips and tongue. Once he's sated, he sinks back with another curse and I close my eyes, licking my lips, swallowing the mess.

I lie on top of Ilmari, Jake curled over my back, their dicks still inside me. My breathing is ragged, my brain in pieces, body numb. Like a raw nerve, there's nothing left to feel. They've wrung me dry.

After a few long moments where we all just breathe, Jake slips out of me with a groan, flopping down to Ilmari's side. His chest heaves from the exertion as he catches his breath. "So fucking good," he says on a sigh. "Best sex ever. Fuck, I love you guys so much, even if I'm not your emergency contact."

Caleb recovers his wits, helping me shift off Ilmari. His cock slips free and I whimper, feeling the gush of cum that leaks from my spent pussy. God its filthy and perfect and so sacred I could cry. It's us, and nothing could be more beautiful.

Caleb lays me on Ilmari's other side, my boneless body curling up against his warm heat. Ilmari puts a protective arm around me, eyes closed as he breathes. Now it's Caleb on his knees between Ilmari's legs, gazing down at us.

"Mars, tell me to stop," he says, heat burning in his eyes. "Tell me you don't want this."

I hold my breath as I glance up at Ilmari.

Ilmari holds Caleb's gaze. Slowly, his other arm reaches out to wrap around Jake's shoulder. He pulls Jake to his side in a quiet gesture of possession. Jake lets himself be pulled, his eyes just as wide as mine. As Caleb watches, Ilmari kisses first my brow, then Jake's. "Take it," he says at last. "It's yours."

Caleb spares a glance for Jake, waiting.

I look at him too, heart in my throat.

Slowly, Jake turns, brushing a kiss against the bare skin of Ilmari's chest. He looks back at Caleb. "Take it, baby. Get your mouth on that dick and tell me how good I taste."

With a groan, Caleb sinks down, one hand holding Ilmari's half-hard dick as he covers his tip with his mouth. The three of us watch as Caleb gives Ilmari a sultry post-orgasm blowjob. Slow and sensual, Caleb savors him with needy sounds. And Ilmari doesn't go soft. No, our Viking hockey god just gets hard again. He groans, his hand coming around to squeeze my breast as he closes his eyes, head arching back.

I can't tear my eyes away as I watch Caleb take him deep. He's loving this. They both are. It's intimate, close, heartfelt. I lose the ability to breathe when Jake slips out from under Ilmari's arm, shimmying down his side to join Caleb.

As I watch, my men taste Ilmari together, teasing his shaft and tip with their tongues, worshipping the cock that just filled me with cum. My heart is going to burst. I can't stand it. I can't leave them to take this step alone. With a desperate whine, I scoot down Ilmari's side, eager to join them.

"Christ—" Ilmari cries out, his hands gripping to the

couch as he holds his hips still, letting the three of us tease him together.

Jake and I taste his shaft as Caleb sucks his tip. Ever the dom, Caleb grabs us by the hair, holding tight as we tease our groaning Finn.

"I'm coming—*fuck*—"

Caleb lifts off Ilmari's tip as Ilmari's cum hits his mouth. It drips back down his shaft. Jake and I groan as we taste him, the three of us united in sharing this gift he's granting us. When it's over, Caleb pulls me in by my hair, kissing me deep. Then he pulls Jake in, kissing him with equal passion. Beneath us, a spent Ilmari watches us through hooded eyes, his chest heaving.

Caleb and Jake break apart and Caleb gazes up Ilmari's body to his face. "Ours," he says, his hands are now protectively holding to me and Jake.

Ilmari nods, sitting up. His hands lift to rest on our opposite shoulders, staking his claim on us. "Yours. I'm yours."

Seizing my moment, I smile. "I'm changing my emergency contact."

Three pairs of eyes glare at me.

"To who?" Jake says as Caleb says, "Why?"

I smile at Jake. "You want to be the first to know? Fine by me. You should get a call in the morning with a pretty important update. Be sure to tell the others, yeah?"

"What update?" he says, eyes wide.

Ilmari and Caleb are both watching me too, confused.

I was planning to wait and do this after we got back from Seattle because I didn't want to steal Harrison's thunder. But you know what? In this moment, the timing feels pretty fucking perfect. And my boys are good at keeping secrets. This will be a Team Price exclusive.

"They had to move my ultrasound appointment next week from Tuesday to Thursday," I say. "Does that work for you, angel? Thursday at 2:30?"

Before he can respond, I get to my feet and start to walk away.

I can practically hear the moment three brains explode behind me. And then I'm laughing, racing into the kitchen, my men hot on my heels.

3

UP IN THE AIR

RACHEL

A jolt of turbulence wakes me and my only feeling is relief. I was having the worst dream. *Again.* I think I was reliving the time Harrison and I got lost at Disneyland. Only, instead of me being the lost kid, I was my mom and *my* kids were lost. I was running around Adventureland like it was an obstacle course, heart racing, palms sweating, panic so sharp I could taste it on my tongue—

Stop.

I take a deep breath, shifting in my seat with my eyes still closed. My arms unfold from under my breasts and I smooth my hands over my growing bump. As soon as I finished my first trimester, the weird dreams started. Normally, I never remember my dreams. Now my visions are flooded nightly with these surrealist hellscapes. And all of them feature in some way me being a terrible mother.

Get pregnant, they said. *It'll be fun*, they said.

I sigh, opening my eyes. We're winging our way home from our latest string of West Coast games. The cabin of the plane is dark, shades pulled. Everything is quiet as the guys get some much needed sleep. The only light comes from the softly glowing call buttons above our heads. It must be really late...or really early.

I glance to my right. Jake and Cay are passed out. Their armrest is flipped up, and Cay is sleeping on Jake's chest, Jake's arm around him. They're curled into each other, limbs entangled, as they try to get comfortable. Half of Cay's face is buried in the blanket, but Jake's is turned my direction, his lips parted slightly as he breathes in and out. His headphones sit askew on his head.

I smile. He played an amazing game last night. He even got a goal assist. He's been on fire for weeks now. There's buzz that when Sully retires next year, the team might give Jake the captain's "C." He'd make a great captain. The guys all love him. And a leadership position would give him a new focus, a new challenge.

Not that our life isn't about to be challenging enough. I look down, brushing my hand over my little bump. Pregnant at twenty-nine and I don't know who the father is. My smile widens as I focus on my thin stack of wedding rings. I *do* know who the father is. The father is Jake...and Caleb...*and* Ilmari.

We plan to do a paternity test once the baby is born. Not because we care about who the biological father is, but because it may allow us more legal protections. I'm married to Ilmari, so if this baby is Jake's or Caleb's, I can list them on the birth certificate.

You'd think this would be an easier process. We can't possibly be the first family in history to have multiple parents involved. If I had my way, I would list all three of my guys on the birth certificate. I'd marry them all too. Legally. We did the informal wedding, but it would be nice if the government would just let me validate my commitment to Jake and Caleb too.

I shift in my seat, rolling my tight shoulders. All this plane travel gets old quick. And we're only halfway through the season.

"Rakas," Ilmari murmurs. "You are well?"

He's a light sleeper, so me shifting in my seat probably woke him up. I turn to face him with a soft smile. He's wearing a Rays hoodie with the hood pulled up, casting his handsome face in shadows. A small number thirty-one is printed over his chest.

"M'fine," I reply.

"You're uncomfortable," he says, reading me like a book. He flips up our armrest and pulls me to him, nestling me against his chest. He's so broad and warm, my own Finnish furnace. His large hand brushes up and down my back as he leans down to kiss my head, propping himself up against the window. "Can't sleep?"

I nuzzle into him, my arm draping around his waist. "I *was* asleep..."

He sighs, his hand stopping its movement. "The dreams again?"

"It's fine," I say, pushing off his thigh with my hand to lean away.

I've been trying to keep my weirdness to myself, but I've woken up more than once twisting up in the sheets or crying out in a panic, so my guys caught on pretty quick that something was wrong. You don't know determined until you've lived with three men desperate to cure you of your pregnancy-induced nightmares. I can't complain if it means I'm now getting served cups of chamomile tea bedside. Nightly hand and foot massages are also now a requirement. Oh, and my side of the bed is fluffed with enough soft blankets and pillows to induce hibernation.

But all of that waits for me at home, which is still thousands of miles away. Up here in the air, I just have to tough it out like everyone else.

Ilmari sighs, following me as I sit up in my seat. It can't be that much longer. Maybe I'll just read for a little while.

"You need to rest," he says. I feel his breath warm against my cheek. That softly spiced smell of his cologne fills my senses, telling me I'm home. But even his presence isn't enough to totally wash away the feelings evoked in the dream.

"I'm too wired to sleep," I reply.

Too freaked. Too upset.

Yeah, we'll stick with wired.

His large hand drops down to cover my little bump. My heart flutters, even as I feel my pulse settle. He's here. He's with us, holding us, protecting us. I rest my hand over his, basking in his warmth, my thumb tracing circles on his skin.

To know the way this man loves this baby, to watch him melt at every doctor's appointment—it's my new addiction. The first time we heard the heartbeat, I figured Jake would cry. I *knew* I would. We weren't prepared for Ilmari. It's the first time I've ever seen him get misty eyed, let alone cry fat tears. Safe to say my mascara didn't survive that first ultrasound.

And now Ilmari's protector mode is off the freakin' charts. You'd think I morphed overnight into a Fabergé egg. Jake had to physically restrain Ilmari when Morrow accidentally elbowed me on the stairs while boarding our last flight. Poor Morrow was falling over himself with apologies while Jake held our brooding goalie back.

"What happened in the dream?" he murmurs, his hand brushing softly back and forth over my bump.

I sigh, leaning my temple against his forehead. "It's silly.

It was just a dream. Or like, a twisted memory or something," I say, trying to brush the whole thing off.

"It's not silly to me," he replies. "I can feel your worry. I see it here," he says, lifting his hand from my stomach to trace his finger over my furrowed brow. "Talk to me, Rakas. Your burdens are mine to carry, remember?"

I nod, swallowing down that thick lump of emotion in my throat. "It's always the same," I say, not daring to look at him. "Every night, I fail them or lose them...or they run away. I can't hold on. Can't be what they need. I'll mess everything up—"

"Shh," he murmurs, his thumb brushing my cheek. "No, my love."

Shit, when did I start crying?

I sniff, blinking my eyes to stop more tears from falling.

"You will be such a wonderful mother," he says, his breath warm against my cheek. "Mun Leijona, I cannot wait to see how you will care for this little one," he adds, his hand back on the bump. "You will be the best mother." As he speaks, he splays his hand proudly against me. He kisses my cheek, his lips soft, even as his beard tickles.

I lean into him, letting the cadence of his voice calm me.

"You are my beating heart, Rakas," he goes on. "Soon it will split in two. This life you carry will take half of me away from you. I've never been a father. I have no example to follow, but I'm not afraid. We lead with love, yes?"

I nod as he leans in closer, kissing me again. "I don't want to mess this up," I say, voice catching.

"We will make mistakes," he replies solemnly. "But between the four of us, this child will know nothing but love. May it have your courage and Caleb's strength, Jake's unwavering kindness—"

"And your patience," I add, turning slightly to face him, my hand splaying over the thirty-one on his chest.

He nods, holding my gaze.

"Mä rakastan sua," I say, my heart overflowing with love for this gentle man.

He cups my face, kissing me softly, his lips caressing mine. "I hate that you have these bad dreams," he murmurs, resting his forehead against mine. "Would that I could crawl inside your mind and root them out. I feel helpless—"

"Kulta—"

"I do," he says, his voice almost a growl. "You are my wife. I must fight your fears."

"Ilmari," I sigh, kissing his cheek. "I love you so much. In your arms, I'm not afraid."

"Then never leave them," he urges. "Stay with me, Rakas. Be mine always."

"Always," I reply, kissing him again.

We sink into each other, kissing slowly, our tongues teasing as our lips press softly. It's a subtle dance. Nothing rushed. I drop my hands to my waist, unbuckling my seat belt so I can shift my hip to turn into him.

His hand smooths along my thigh, his thumb like iron as he follows the line of my muscle. "Let me help you," he murmurs against my lips.

"Help?" I echo, distracted as I tug his hood back, letting my fingers brush over the buzzed nape of his neck.

"You're stressed," he replies, kissing along my jaw. "Worried about things we cannot control," he adds, teasing the lobe of my ear. "Unable to sleep when you're tired. Unable to stop the torrent of your thoughts."

I sigh into him, feeling the effect he has on my entire body. Warmth pools low in my stomach, spiraling out until I feel even the tips of my fingers buzzing. "Ilmari, please—"

My words end on a sharp intake of breath as he shifts his hand down to cup between my legs. Warmth radiates from my center.

"Please, my love. Let me ease you."

He wants to do this here? Now?

I've thought of this scenario a thousand times before. Who doesn't imagine joining the mile high club when you're sitting next to a specimen as fine as my 6'5" tatted, bearded Viking of a husband?

But we've never tried anything. He's too protective. The idea of one of his teammates seeing anything, hearing anything—it would probably make him go full King Kong and start tearing up the seats.

I look in his eyes. "Ilmari—"

He ducks between us, picking up the blanket that slipped off my lap while I slept. Draping it over me, he taps my right knee. "Lift this up."

I instantly know what he has in mind. We can use my leg as a kind of tent. No one has to see a thing. With a smile, I shift my angle and prop up my foot on the seat, my knee pressing gently against the seat in front of me.

His right arm goes around my shoulders, pulling me to him, as his left slips under the blanket. He smooths his hand over my growing little bump. "My wife," he growls possessively.

"Yours," I say, breathless.

"You are a queen among men, Rakas," he says, his voice softening as he dips his hand lower, his fingers smoothing over the top of my waistband. "A lioness. The steady rock on which our foundations are built. No more fear." He kisses my lips, his hand slipping inside my leggings. "No worry."

I already feel strung out, my pussy desperate for his touch. "No worry," I echo.

His fingers seek, the first and third parting me open as the second slides over my clit. He bites back a groan, his face dropping to nuzzle my neck. "How I long to put you on my lap and have you ride my cock."

"Yes," I sigh, my left hand curling around to cup his neck as I lean into him, keeping my legs spread.

"I would bury myself in you, wife. No beginning. No end."

"Please," I gasp, my voice barely audible.

He works me slow, almost teasingly so, his finger sliding up and down from my clit to the entrance of my pussy. Just as he presses in with his finger, letting one knuckle dip inside, he pulls out, trailing up to circle my clit again. It's torturous. And he's not giving me anything like the pressure I crave.

"Kulta, please—"

"Breathe," he murmurs, his face nuzzling mine. "Focus on what you feel. Get out of your own head. Just breathe with me."

I take a deep breath, letting myself sink closer against him as his hand continues to move, teasing and caressing me. It's sensual and maddening at the same time. But I just breathe, letting him touch me how he wants.

He starts to sink his finger in deeper, curling it against my inner wall. I'm fighting the urge to moan and he knows it. His right hand shifts around my shoulder as he buries two fingers inside me, his right hand covering my mouth as I gasp.

"Quiet," he murmurs in my ear. "Your sounds are only for me."

I breathe over his hand, eyes sinking closed as he fingers me, driving me wild. Now I'm fighting the urge to move with him. My hips want to rock. I want to ride his hand. Sitting still is its own kind of odd thrill. I'm just letting this happen to me. I'm not participating at all. It's strange and exciting. Ilmari is in total control.

The hand over my mouth shifts, the pad of his finger brushing my bottom lip, and I know what he wants. I part my lips in invitation and he sinks his finger into my mouth. I suck, nipping with my teeth and teasing with my tongue, until I earn a muttered, "Fuck."

He redoubles his efforts to drive me wild, dipping in and circling my clit. He leads me right up to that edge, then walks back. As I pant under his hand, he adds a second finger in my mouth. I suck harder, biting back a moan. He sinks the fingers of his left hand back inside my desperate pussy, his thumb working my clit. Finally, he's giving me the pressure I crave.

"Yes," I whimper, the sound garbled as he pulls his fingers from my mouth. I'm panting for air. The ache feels good. It helps me center. It gets me out of my head.

Just when I'm about to come, his hand grips tightly to my jaw. "Wait," he hisses in my ear.

I whine, despite for release. "Ilmari—"

He jerks my head, turning me so I'm facing the aisle.

I gasp, eyes wide, as I take in two pairs of eyes watching us from the opposite seats. As if they could sense what we were doing, Caleb and Jake are awake. Their dark gazes are enough to take the fire in my blood and turn it into a raging inferno. I swallow my needy moan.

There's no holding it back. I come. *Hard.* I don't know if I've ever soundlessly come with one of my guys before. The need to be silent adds a new layer to the orgasm, rocking my entire body, sending me into aftershocks that leave me trembling all over.

I quiver in Ilmari's hold, my eyes locked on Jake and

Caleb across the aisle. My pussy squeezes his fingers and I double down, my breath ragged as I ride it out. Once I'm spent, I relax in his arms, biting my bottom lip as the post-orgasm high has me floating back down into my seat.

"Beautiful," Ilmari murmurs in my ear.

Before I can stop him, he's slipping his arm from around my shoulders as he tugs his left hand from my leggings. I shift, righting myself. Ilmari unbuckles his seatbelt.

"What are you—"

"Let me out," he says softly.

I drop my leg back to the floor and curl my knees in, giving him enough space to slip past me. He stands in the aisle, his tall frame towering over me. As I peer up at him, he stretches, cracking his neck. Then he shifts on his feet, inching closer to the other side of the aisle.

My gaze drops down his face to his shoulder. I follow the line of his left arm into the shadows of Jake and Cay's seats. Without looking down, Ilmari offers out his hand to them, splaying the two fingers that were just in my cunt in a "V."

"Oh god," I whimper, my pussy clenching tight. As I watch, Jake and Cay lean forward, each sucking one of his wet fingers into their mouths, their cheeks all but pressed together. Just like that, I'm ready to come again.

They pop off him and Ilmari wordlessly taps Jake's shoulder. He knows him well enough to know what Jake needs now. What we *both* need. Jake unbuckles lightning fast, slipping out of his seat. He does a quick adjust, even though no one can see him with his body angled in toward Ilmari.

Their chests brush as Ilmari turns and drops down into his empty aisle seat. Then Jake climbs nimbly over my legs, sinking into Ilmari's window seat.

Meanwhile Caleb is already turning away, his head

45

resting against the bulkhead. I'm sure he'll be asleep again in minutes. When we get home, he'll corner me somewhere in the house and fuck me from behind until I scream. I'm already looking forward to it.

But Jake needs more and he can't wait. He's hardly touched the seat before he's pulling me to him. "Come here, baby," he murmurs.

I snuggle in close. My post-orgasm bliss is leaving me warm and relaxed, which was Ilmari's goal. All my guys are great with aftercare, especially when our play gets hot and heavy. But Jake is just too Taurus to function. And now that I'm pregnant? Forget about it. If he had his way, I'd be wrapped in silk and feathers and carried around on a palanquin. I haven't put the idea past him yet. What else are rookies for but to carry the soon-to-be-captain's wife from the gym to the practice rink?

But he doesn't need sex from me now. He just needs connection. Of all my guys, he's the only one who never sleeps alone. Caleb wanders in and out of our rooms like a cat all the time. Even Ilmari will sometimes sleep in a separate room when he's in his head about an upcoming game or struggling with his mild bouts of insomnia. But never Jake.

From the moment we all said 'I do' in my dad's LA living room, he's been resolute in his desire to sleep by my side every night. The away schedule is hard, because the players have to sleep alone. Even being legally married to Cay, rules are rules. We've broken that particular rule on more than one occasion, but we generally try to be good.

Thank goodness there's no rules about sitting together on the plane. So now I press in against him, letting him adjust the blanket on my lap, tugging it up to cover my shoulder.

His hand drops down to fan over my baby bump. "Nugget okay?"

"Mhmm," I murmur into his chest, my eyes already feeling droopy.

He kisses my forehead as I fist his sweatshirt. I curl my body into him, determined to share his skin. I'm not sure if he asks me any more questions, and I doubt I answer. I'm a leaf on the breeze, floating off into a dreamless sleep.

4

IKEA

ILMARI

"Ilmari? You home?"

Poseidon barks, and I jolt upright. My phone slips off my chest, clattering to the floor. I glance around the dark living room, my eyes pausing on the wall of glass. Outside, a blanket of grey clouds hang heavy and low. Spring in Florida. Cool and rainy, just the way I like it.

I arrived home from practice as the first drops began to fall. When I got inside, the house was empty, which is a rarity. Given our differing schedules, someone is almost always home. Exhausted from a full-body workout, I slid open the glass door and dropped onto the sofa, content to listen to the rain.

Clearly, I must have fallen asleep.

With a groan, I roll to my side, snatching my phone off the floor. My whole body hurts. I'm getting too old for this. The season is nearly over and playoffs are about to begin. Is it wrong of me to secretly hope we don't advance?

I stretch and yawn, cracking my neck.

"Oh—sorry, babe," Rachel calls from the kitchen, setting

her shopping bags down. The dog dances excitedly around her feet. "Were you asleep?"

"It's fine," I reply, checking the time. Nearly five o'clock. I was asleep for almost two hours. No one came home in all that time? Odd. "Where are the others?"

She's busy moving around the kitchen, opening and shutting cabinets. "Umm...I think they were meeting up with Novy and Morrow for a quick bite."

I get up from the sofa, doing another stretch. Every muscle feels tight. I'll sit in the sauna after dinner. Maybe I can convince Jake to give me a massage tonight. He's damn good at them. But he always demands a string of favors in payment. Last time he made me walk the dog for a week.

"Do you have any plans tonight?" Rachel calls.

I step around the end of the sofa and move towards the kitchen, pausing to take in this side view of my wife. Rachel's long, brown hair tumbles down her back as she lifts up on her toes, reaching for a high shelf of the cabinet. Her pregnant belly presses against the counter and she winces.

"Let me," I say, rushing to her side. The dog skitters out of my way.

"Last one," she replies with a smile, handing me the glass.

I go to take it, but she holds on, our fingers brushing as she reels me in. Our lips press together in a quick kiss. Stepping in next to her, I easily set the glass on the shelf.

"Say, since you're so strong and soooo good at being helpful..."

I pause, glancing over my shoulder. She's wearing *that* look. The look she gets when she's about to ask me to do something she knows I don't want to do. It's equal parts pleading and seductive, like she'll beg me to fuck her and then I'll be the one thanking her.

"What do you want?" I say, my tone laced with obstinance. I can't help myself. She says it's because I'm an Aries. I know it's because I'm Finn.

She steps in closer, establishing touch. Her hands stroke up my forearms, her thumb brushing over where her name is tattooed on my skin. Her rounded belly, heavy with our child, presses in at my hip. I groan, fighting her pull. But it's hopeless. She is the sea siren and I her weary sailor, destined to crash upon her rocks.

"I need your help," she says, her voice an alluring murmur. "I can't do it on my own. Not in this condition," she adds, one hand brushing over her belly.

My senses fill with her scent, the feel of her, the magnetic pull I still feel every time she's close. She's not fighting fair. I pull my arms gently loose of her grip. "Just tell me, Rakas."

With a smirk, she drops her siren act, her voice returning to normal. "I need you to go to IKEA with me."

My arousal sinks like a lead balloon. "Fuck. Tonight?"

"Come on," she laughs, placing her hands on my shoulders. "It won't be that bad. In and out. I just need to pick up a bookcase for the baby's room. And unless you want me lifting heavy boxes—"

"No," I growl. "My eight-months-pregnant wife will not be lifting bookcases. I thought we already had one," I add. It's not a question. I *know* we have a bookcase in the baby's room. I put it together.

"Yeah, but have you seen the way all the books are stacking up? I swear, if Tess buys us one more, we could open our own library."

"If you tell me what you want, I'll go get it," I say, smoothing my hands up her sides. "There's no need for you to go. Stay here and rest."

She pulls away with a pout. "But I wanna go. You're the one who doesn't like IKEA."

"There's too many people," I reason. "And the aisles are too narrow. And last time that ruffian slammed his cart into your ankle." My mind floods with the memory of her crying out in pain. She dropped her soda on the floor and we had to find a staff member to go get a mop.

She laughs, waving me off. "Yeah, that hurt like a bitch. But that was *one* time. I very much doubt that kid will be there again. And if he is, I'll let you punch him in the head, okay?"

I grumble, knowing she doesn't mean it. She never lets me do violence on her behalf.

"Besides, you know how much we all love their little chocolate cookies," she teases. Then she's leaning in, trailing a soft finger down the bridge of my nose. "And if you're *very* good...and you don't complain about the crowds even once..." She tips up on her toes and whispers in my ear, "I'll buy you a jar of lingonberry jam."

I smirk. "You don't play fair."

"I have three super competitive husbands," she replies with a shrug. "I play to win. Carry my coffee while I shop, and I'll put some of that jam on my nipples when we get home and let you lick it off."

Now we're both laughing as I shake my head. "Fuck," I say, knowing my evening plans have been made for me. "I love you. Even when you manipulate me with your feminine wiles. Especially then," I add for good measure.

"I know," she replies with a satisfied smile. "Now go put a shirt on. This show is not for public viewing," she adds, gesturing at my bare chest.

With a patient sigh, I go in search of my lost shirt. And I feel like I had socks on at one point too...

EMILY RATH

. . .

"See? This is fine," Rachel says for the third time, leading the way through the IKEA kitchen showroom.

I say nothing, walking dutifully at her side, holding her decaf caramel latte. Why do I need to confirm what we both can see? This is a slow night. There's hardly anyone else here.

I tried convincing Rachel to take the shortcut straight through to the fulfillment center, but she insists that IKEA is an "experience." My wife is nearly nine months pregnant with our child. If she wants to wander IKEA on a Thursday night looking at sofa beds and closet organizers, I will hold her coffee.

But she seems a bit unsettled tonight. She usually likes to take her time, sitting in every chair, and we never escape without at least one new kitchen gadget. Tonight, she hardly seems to spare the showrooms a glance. I watch as she peers around, almost as if she's expecting to see someone she knows around every corner.

I follow her gaze before glancing down at her. "Are you well?"

"Mhmm," she replies, snatching her hot coffee from my hand. "Yep. Never better."

"The baby—"

"Has two more weeks left in the oven," she replies, cutting me off with a stern look. Her sandals slap as she walks with purpose through the mattress section. She's practically marching.

My irritation simmers. "At some point you will slow down, yes?" I call after her. It takes nothing to catch up with her on my longer legs. "You will realize you're about to have a baby and let us care for you?"

This gets her attention and she slows her pace, one hand on her rounded belly as she glances up at me. "You *do* care for me," she says with a gentle smile. "All three of you have been amazing. You spoil me silly."

I frown. "We'd spoil you *more* if you'd sit down for ten minutes together."

She hands her coffee back to me with a sigh. "Tomorrow is my last day before maternity leave. And I've hardly lifted a finger at work for the past month anyway. Doc Tyler and Hillary fuss over me like a pair of mother hens. The only one who doesn't treat me like I'm made of glass is Poppy. And the three of you are even worse once I get home—"

"Because you're pregnant—"

"Yeah, *pregnant*," she huffs, hands on her hips. Her beautiful dark eyes flash with annoyance. "I'm not sick, and I'm not dying. In fact, this here—" She waves a hand at her belly. "This is a sign of me *thriving*, Ilmari. I'm perfectly healthy. Lil Baby No Name is healthy too. I'm as strong as ever and just as capable."

"Don't we know it," I mutter.

She flashes me a grin. "Besides," she says, her voice suddenly louder. "I didn't hear you complaining last night when I was deep-throating you in the shower—"

"Saatana, Rakas," I grumble, wrapping an arm around her and pulling her to my side as she laughs. "You want everyone to know our business?"

She snorts, pulling my hand from her mouth and lacing our fingers together. "Come on, Bear Man. Don't forget our deal about the jam either," she adds with a backwards glance, batting her lashes.

I shake my head with a sigh, following at her side.

As we walk in silence through the children's section, my bullshit meter starts to buzz. She's not stopping. My wife has

EMILY RATH

no interest in looking at baby furniture? Rachel "Look How Tiny and Cute" Price isn't trying to convince me we need a child's wooden kitchen set? No heated discussion over adding another stuffed animal to the menagerie?

"Rakas," I mutter, pulling her to a halt. "What is going on—"

"Fuck. Alright, fine," she huffs. Her entire demeanor changes. She's no longer holding my hand, she's clinging to it. Her dark eyes go wide as she gazes up at me. Her nerves set me on edge.

"Rakas, what—"

"I said I'd go along with this, but now I'm panicking," she says. "Please know how much we all love you, okay? And if you'll just let this happen, I'll do anything you want, baby. I'm serious. *Anything*. Pick your kinkiest fantasy—"

"Rakas—"

"Or chores," she says. "I'll get on my knees and scrub every baseboard with soap and water. I'll clean your hockey gear for a month—"

"*Rachel*," I growl, hands on her shoulders. I lower my face closer to hers. "Breathe...then talk to me. What's wrong?"

She sucks in a breath, holding it in her cheeks. She lets it out in a puff. "Nothing," she says, shaking her head. "Nothing is wrong. Just know we all love you so damn much." But I know she's lying. It looks like holding in the truth is about to make her pop like a balloon.

"Rachel—"

"Just come on," she says, pulling me along. "And remember that, while I may be complicit, I was definitely not the mastermind."

My heart stops as my brain catches up.

Oh fuck. She can't mean...

54

We step around the corner into the café and—

"HAPPY BIRTHDAY!!!"

I jolt to a halt, confronted by a massive crowd of people shouting all at once. Every single person I know in this city seems to be crowded inside this IKEA. The entire Rays team, their wives and kids, support staff, our neighbors. I even see my favorite barista from the local coffee shop wearing a party hat and blowing a noisemaker.

Above their heads, a massive banner reads "Happy Birthday, Mars!" There are balloons, kids shouting and running, noise poppers...and I'm the center of attention. This is my personal hell. I feel frozen.

Next to me, Rachel squeezes my hand. "You still alive?" she asks, peering up at me. "Remember, I had—"

"Nothing to do with this. Yes, I know," I say, recovering my breath. I squeeze her hand in reassurance.

The guys all surge forward and there's one face in the lead wearing a sly grin.

"This was allll my idea!" Jake shouts, wrapping me in a big hug. "I fucking love you, man."

"I know," I say, just letting it happen. There'll be no stopping him at this point. Why fight it?

"Dude, he's fuckin' pissed," Novy says with a laugh.

"Told you he would be," says Morrow. "Hey, man. Happy birthday," he adds, cuffing my shoulder.

Jake lets me go, turning his attention to Rachel. He wraps her in a quick embrace. "I can't believe that actually worked. You were so surprised," he says at me.

"Shoulda seen your face," Davidson laughs, taking a sip of his fizzy water.

"I was sure you'd break and give us all away," Jake teases Rachel.

"I nearly did," she replies, and they all laugh.

Jake slings an arm around my shoulder, pulling me forward. "Come on, old man. Come check out your party."

I glance around at all the decorations, noting the faces of the bemused IKEA staff, all wandering around in their blue and yellow-striped shirts. "Jake, you know I'm Finnish—"

"Fuck's sake, Mars," he grumbles. "*Yes*, I know. Everyone knows. That house plant knows," he adds, pointing at a fake plant on the table. "But Finland doesn't have a furniture superstore with an in-store cafeteria that sells enough salmon and broccoli to feed this crowd. And I looked it up," he adds, pulling me forward and pointing up at the colorful menu signs. "Everything here is stuff you eat in Finland too. And look at the balloons," he adds with another point. "Blue and white only. No yellow. I was *very* strict about that."

I can't help but smile, shaking my head.

Langley steps in, slipping a shiny blue party hat on my head. "Happy Birthday, Mars."

"The cafeteria is ours for the night," Jake says with a wave of his hand. "Swedish meatballs and salmon for everyone!" He says this loud enough for those around to cheer. Then he leans in, his arm tightening around my shoulders. "And I'm sorry, but the desserts here are total shit, so I got some good cake. It's over there. And the present table is over there," he adds, pointing in opposite directions.

I glance between the partygoers and spy see a table piled high with colorful gifts. "Christ—"

Music starts up in the corner and the crowd cheers again. Jake brought a DJ to the IKEA?

Kids run around as Jake keeps me in his orbit, forcing me to make the rounds and greet all my guests. I quickly lose track of Rachel as she flits around too, hugging wives.

Before long, I find myself seated at a table, surrounded by Rays. Jake sweeps up behind me and sets a plate down

with a flourish. It's an IKEA plate of salmon, mashed pota-
toes, and steamed vegetables. There's a candle shoved into
the salmon fillet. The tip flickers with warm, golden light. As
the crowd all surges around me, the Rays closest lead
everyone in a chaotic chorus of 'Happy Birthday.' I blow the
candle out to boisterous cheers.

"Happy birthday, man," Jake says, leaning down to speak
in my ear, both hands squeezing my shoulders. "We love
you." He pecks my cheek with a friendly kiss before turning
his attention to Davidson sitting at my side. It's a scuffle as
Jake makes him move, saying that spot is reserved for our
pregnant wife. Soon after, Rachel joins us, and I split my
salmon with her. And fuck if the cupcakes aren't damn
delicious.

FOR THE NEXT HOUR, JAKE HARDLY LETS ME OUT OF HIS SIGHT.
I somehow get roped into playing a bag-tossing game called
'cornhole.' When the forwards start taking the game too
seriously, it only takes a few carefully placed bad throws on
my part to get booted.

I make my escape for the bathroom, as much in search
of a moment's peace as I am a place to relieve myself. I'm
washing my hands at the sink when the door creaks open. I
glance up to see Caleb walk in.

He pauses just inside the door, arms crossed over his
chest. He's wearing a satisfied smirk, like he knows how
much this is killing me. I've hardly seen him all night. He's
kept to the edges of the party, quietly standing back or
helping the staff clear plates.

"How badly do you wanna leave?"

"It's fine," I say, lathering my hands with soap.

He takes a few steps closer. "You say the word, and I'll

get you out of here. There's an 'employee only' corridor just outside that will take us out to the front. I know. I checked."

We exchange a smirk. "Appreciated, but unnecessary."

His smile dips slightly. "Why are you so okay with all this?"

I just shrug. "It's important to Jake."

He nods, closing the distance between us, his hip leaning against the sink. "Jake loves you," he says, glancing at my reflection in the mirror, rather than at me. "That's what this is. This terrible party is because he loves you."

"I know."

"He just wants you to see how much you're loved. By the team, by Jax. He wanted to surround you with the faces of everyone who thinks well of you."

"I know," I say again.

"So...you're not mad?"

I glance over my shoulder at him. His expression is impossible to read. "Why would I be mad?"

"Because this party is your literal hell."

"Maybe," I say with a smile. "But I know he means well."

"He does." Caleb slips his hand into his back pocket, pulling out an envelope. With a sigh he holds it out to me.

"What's this?" I say, drying my hands on my pants before I take it.

"The other half of your gift. He coordinated us. Jake wanted this party to be from him. And this is supposed to be from me," he adds, gesturing at the envelope. "But they're both from Jake."

I glance down at the envelope. "Should I open it now?"

He shrugs. "Whatever you want. It's yours either way."

I open it, slipping out the few folded papers inside.

"It's a trip to the Grand Canyon," he says before I can finish reading the top of what is apparently the receipt for airline tickets. "Jake planned the whole thing," he adds. "For just the five of us."

I glance up. "Five?"

"Yeah, he wants it to be Nugget's first family vacation."

I smile, glancing back down at the papers.

"He knows how badly you've wanted to see it. He planned the whole thing. Sunrise hot air balloon, river cruise, hiking, a spa day. And everything is private. No crowds. No hockey. Just the desert air in your hair. And just us. Just family."

I nod, emotion thick in my throat. "It's perfect," I say, folding the papers and slipping them back inside the envelope. I glance over at Caleb again. "Why did he make you give this to me?"

Caleb shrugs, hands in his pockets. "I think he wanted me to come across as the thoughtful one. You know, for balance."

"I have no recollection of ever discussing the Grand Canyon with Jake," I admit, fighting my smile.

"I'm sure you have," he mutters.

"I'm sure I haven't," I reply, folding my arms over my chest to mirror his stance. "I *have* discussed it with you. Several times. You gave him the idea, didn't you?"

He shrugs again. "He wanted my opinion. You're just lucky he went with this one, because my other recommendation was Disney World," he adds with a grin.

I groan, picturing the five of us wandering Disney World getting stopped every ten feet by someone who wants to take a picture. You'd think after two years the public's interest in us would wane. We've all learned to weather it, but a private vacation with just us and no outside eyes feels perfect.

"Thank you, Caleb."

He nods. "Happy Birthday, Mars." He glances over his shoulder towards the door. "We should probably head back out there. Don't wanna deprive this party of it's shining star."

I laugh, even as inside I feel a flutter of confusion deep in my gut. There's also a flicker of recognition from my newest full-time companion: doubt.

The truth is that I've become tired of the spotlight. Tired of the press events. Of answering questions about my health and fitness to play, dissecting all my bad saves and making vague promises about future games. I'm tired of the endless travel, the spinning carousel of home and away games. I'm tired of living out of suitcases and missing my wife so much I can't breathe.

I'm just tired.

In body.

In spirit.

And our lives are all about to change in such a seismic way. The birth of this child will alter everything. For Rachel—her ability to travel with us, her ability to work, at least at first. For the three of us too. Managing four careers with a child will be difficult to say the least. Caleb is integral to the working of the Rays. I know they're eyeing him for a promotion to lead Equipment Manager. And Rachel is only a year into her new Assistant Director role. Jake is on fire, playing the best he has in his career.

And here I stand, barely holding myself together—

"Hey," Caleb murmurs, his hand on my shoulder. "You okay?"

I glance down, following the line of his arm to his face. "Hmm?"

"I lost you there," he says, his brows lowered over his dark eyes. "You went deep in your head. What's up?"

I've been holding these feelings inside me for weeks. Months. If I was going to tell anyone, it would be Caleb. Jake would try to fix everything and Rachel would take it on as her burden to bear. Caleb will just listen. He'll let me deal with it in my way.

He inches closer, his hand sliding from my shoulder, down my arm. Outside of sex, it's rare that he touches me. I'm not ashamed to admit that I like it. His full attention is on me and I feel warm. Safe. Protected.

"Hey," he says, his voice soft. He's looking at me like no one else exists. "Talk to me."

I open my mouth, ready to tell him how I feel—

BANG.

The door behind him goes flying open and Langley ducks his head inside. "Guys—fuck, there you are," he pants.

Caleb spins around, dropping his hand away from me. "What?"

"It's Rachel. Get the fuck out here."

My heart drops from my chest and I'm practically shoving past Caleb to get to the door. We wedge ourselves out at the same time, barreling down the hall and around the corner back into the café. It's pandemonium.

"Move!" Caleb bellows, pushing forward.

Using my height, I look for her.

"There they are!" Tess calls. "Guys, over here!"

The crowd parts and I see Rachel standing, both hands on her stomach. Jake is next to her, his arm around her shoulders, a panicked look on his face.

"Oh, thank fuck," he calls. "Get over here."

"What's wrong?" says Caleb at the same time I say, "What happened?"

"I'm freaking the fuck out," Jake cries. "I can't deal with this on my own!"

A few people laugh as Rachel rolls her eyes, patting his hand like he's the one in distress. "Angel, I'm fine," she says. Her ready smile eases my panic.

She's fine. This is fine. This is—

"You're not fucking fine," Jake counters. "You're having our baby in an IKEA!" He drags a hand through his hair. "Ohmygod, we're gonna have to name it Flörp or Lörten or something, aren't we?"

"Don't be dramatic," she replies as the wives around him laugh.

But Caleb and I are still in the dark, so none of this is funny. Caleb steps in at her other side. "Someone better tell us what the fuck is going on—"

"She's having the baby," Jake replies.

"No, I'm not," Rachel counters. "Well—I mean, *yes*—Little Flörp Price is coming," she teases. "But we've got time," she adds, looking at me. "My water just broke."

"Oh shit," says Caleb, suddenly breathless.

"Best birthday present ever, eh, big guy?" says J-Lo, elbowing me in the ribs.

For the second time tonight, I feel frozen. This is happening now? We had weeks yet. I had weeks. To decide. To plan. To make my feelings known. I glance to Caleb, hoping he can see the desperation in my eyes. In a blink, the switch in his brain flips and I audibly sigh with relief, knowing he'll take care of everything.

"Right," he barks, stepping away from Rachel. "Party's over, assholes. Novy, Morrow!"

The guys step forward.

"You're on clean-up duty," Caleb orders.

"Got it," says Morrow with a nod.

Caleb steps around Rachel, fishing in Jake's pocket. "J-Lo!"

"Yeah, boss?" he says, stepping forward.

"Get our car home," Caleb replies, tossing him Jake's car keys. "Get the bags by the front door and bring them to the hospital. And—"

"Bring the dog home with me," J-Lo finishes for him. "Consider it done."

"We've got Sy," says his wife, Lauren. "Don't even worry about him. The girls are thrilled to have him."

"Just go," says Langley, stepping in at my other side. "We've got everything covered here, guys. Go have that baby."

The whole party cheers at that, but I barely hear it. My mind is still too busy churning like rapids in a river.

Then Caleb's face floats in front of me. "Help Jake get Hurricane outside. I'll pull the car around."

He turns to leave and I reach out my hand, snatching for his arm. He jerks to a halt, spinning around. "Mars, what—"

"Wait," I say, heart in my throat. I can't do this without him here. I need him. He grounds me in a way the other two can't.

He tugs on his arm, trying to free himself. "Mars—"

"I said, wait," I growl, pulling him forward. I need Rachel too. And Jake. I need my family.

She smiles at my approach, which shows her excitement. But the tightness of her hand as she takes mine belies her nerves. She needs me too. My family needs me.

Kissing her brow, I keep a tight hold on Caleb as I turn, clearing my voice to address the crowd. "Thank you all for coming out tonight," I call.

The room hoots and cheers, everyone wearing wide smiles.

"I've played on many teams in my long career," I go on. "But the Rays are special. This isn't a team, it's a family," I say, glancing at all the faces around the room. "I've been grateful to be part of it."

Many people smile and nod.

I glance to Rachel and Jake, making a decision that will affect the rest of our lives. But I know down to my marrow that it's the right decision. My family needs me now, and I want to be fit enough to be there for them for all the tomorrows we share. They deserve the best of me, not whatever's left when they scrape me off the ice.

"Ilmari..." Rachel murmurs, her hand tightening in mine, and I know she knows.

"Oh shit," Caleb says on my other side. He knows too.

Taking a breath, I call out to the room, "Every moment of my career has been a blessing...but I'm done." My gaze settles on Coach Johnson, standing by the cake table wearing a party hat and a shocked look. "This will be my last season playing professional hockey," I say, looking right at him. "When this season ends, I'm retiring."

Silence follows my words as everyone in the cafeteria sits with my announcement.

The dam finally breaks when Novy calls out, "Let's hear it for Mars Price! Best damn goalie the League has ever seen!"

The cafeteria goes wild, and then everyone is surging forward, hugging and congratulating me. It's chaos. I'm buffeted on all sides as Caleb and Jake protectively pull Rachel back.

It only lasts a minute or two before Jake is back at my side. "Alright, enough!" he barks, waving people back. "We'll throw him a banger of a retirement party this summer. For now, all you assholes better make this place look spotless. I don't want IKEA calling me while I'm at the hospital saying we stole a tray or scuffed the floor."

"We got it, man," says Novy. "Just go—"

"Yeah, before Doc does pop that baby out here and now!"

"At least there's a lot of beds in here—"

"And towels!"

"My wife is *not* having our baby in an IKEA!" Jake shouts. "So everybody get the fuck outta the way!"

That sentence jerks me out of my stupor. "Mitä vittua," I curse. My pregnant wife is in labor in an IKEA, and I'm just standing here making speeches. I let go of Caleb and he takes the hint. He tears off across the café, anxious to bring the car around.

Surging forward, I join Jake in taking Rachel by the hands. She seems in good spirits, her cheeks flushed, her eyes glassy with excitement.

"Good luck!"

"Can't wait to meet Baby Price!"

"Happy Birthday, Mars!"

The crowd wishes us well as we take off, following the IKEA staffer ready to lead us through the shortcut to the front of the store.

"Jeezus fucking Christ," Jake grumbles from Rachel's other side. "You done giving me a heart attack, Mars? You in this now?"

"I'm here," I reply, voice set with determination.

"And you're sure?" Rachel says, glancing up at me. "About the retirement? You don't have to decide anything now—"

"No," I say quickly. The weight in my chest already feels lighter. I can breathe again. "No, it's finished. Hockey is finished for me."

"Shit, I just got goosebumps," Jake says from her other side. "You sure you're sure?"

"I'm done," I say again. "My body is done. I've played enough hockey for ten lifetimes. It's time for a new adventure," I add, gesturing down to Rachel's belly.

Rachel smiles. "Full time daddy? I like it. Though you may come to prefer the hockey."

"Yeah, not to poop on your party, Mars, but tonight's not really about you anymore," says Jake. "Rachel and Nugget upstaged you."

"And I'm sorry for that," she adds quickly, breathing out through pursed lips. "Couldn't be helped though."

"Don't apologize," I say. "You are about to have our child. There is no greater gift one could receive."

Jake just sighs. "And just like that, weeks of planning wasted without such much as a 'thank you, Jake' to be heard."

Rachel laughs again. "We'll have a do-over in a couple months. I can lure Ilmari here under false pretenses again. Maybe next time we'll have a bouncy castle."

She and Jake laugh.

"I have a better idea," I say, an idea spinning in my mind.

They both glance sharply up at me.

"Okay, with that face, even I'm scared," says Jake as Rachel laughs again.

I smile. "Caleb's birthday is in November, yes?"

"Yeeees," Rachel replies, her dark eyes narrowed on me.

"What say we throw him a Rays birthday party weekend at Disney World? Family friendly. All the parks. Plus the water one."

Both Rachel and Jake come to a halt, staring at me. Then their faces split into twin grins.

"You're an evil fucking genius," says Jake.

"He'll hate it so much," Rachel echoes. "Ohmygod— costumes. We can have costumes for each park. *Frozen* and he can be Olaf—"

"Pleeeease dress him as Peter Pan again," Jake laughs. "Fuck me, best idea ever. And I still have so much time to plan. You're amazing, Mars—"

"But baby first," Rachel says, her breath coming out in a little pant. "At this point, I'll agree to anything so long as we get this baby outta me first."

Her wince acts like a shock to our systems and Jake and I switch fully into defense mode. Our wife is in labor. Nothing will stand in our way from getting her safely to the hospital.

"Wait—oh no," Rachel cries, trying to tug us to a halt.

"What?" I growl.

"What's wrong, baby?" Jake echoes.

She glances over her shoulder then looks up at me. "Your lingonberry jam. I left the jar on the table."

"What—jam?" Jake glances between us with a confused frown. "You wanna stop this baby parade over a jar of jam?"

The earnest look in her eyes has me falling in love with her all over again. She's in labor with my child, and yet she's genuinely concerned about misplacing a jar of jam.

Swooping down I kiss her, my hand cupping her face possessively. She sighs into the kiss, one hand clinging to my shirt. I quickly pull away. "Forget the jam," I say. "You're having our baby. Just focus on that now, joo?"

Tears well in her eyes as she finally lets herself feel the intensity of this moment.

"Have this baby for us, and I'll buy you a jar of jam for every day of the week."

Slowly, she nods, sucking in a nervous breath as her hand covers mine. "Yeah."

Jake glances between us, one brow raised. "Yeah?"

"Yeah," I echo.

"Alright. Then let's go, Team Price. We're doin' this. It's baby time." Jake steps in behind us, his hands on both our shoulders as he gives us a little shove. "No more unscheduled stops, or Cay is gonna get creative and set the building on fire just to smoke us out."

As soon as Jake says it, I realize we can't put it past Caleb to take such a drastic measure. Not where Rachel is concerned. "Come," I say, holding tighter to Rachel's hand.

Behind me, I hear the anxiety in Jake's voice as he says, "And we all know I was kidding about the Flörp thing, right? Mars, if this is your baby, *please* don't name him Flörp, okay?"

I smile, glancing over my shoulder at him. "No promises."

"Fuck."

5

PATERNITY TEST

RACHEL

"Come on, you know you can tell me. Do you have a preference?" Tess leans in, propping her elbows on the edge of my hospital bed, as she flashes me a conspiratorial grin.

I just laugh, shaking my head. "You know I don't."

"But if you did," she teases.

I roll my eyes. "Don't make me call the nurse. She'll drag you out by your pretty red curls."

"Fine," she huffs, leaning away. "I mean, I can't win my bet if you won't just tell me...but it's fine."

"Ohmygod," I cry as she laughs. I look around for something to throw at her, but nothing is close enough. "You are *not* taking bets on which of my husbands I want to be the father of my baby, Tess! You know I'm not going to choose."

She snorts, leaning back in her chair. "Girl, just listen to that sentence, and tell me we don't live in some kind of crazy world," she says with a smile, shaking her head.

I play it back in my head, and now I'm smiling too. I guess she has a point. From the outside, I know my life seems unconventional. Very publicly married for three years to three wonderful men. We have a beautiful son. Another is nestled asleep in my arms, newly born.

Of course, the timing could have been a little better. This time last year, I'd just given birth to our sweet Jamie. I was ready to settle into the wonderful and weird life of parenthood. But then I had to go get myself knocked up again less than two months later.

Now it's been over a year and a half of me being perpetually pregnant. Mr. Oops Baby came out early too, suffering a mild case of jaundice. We've been in the hospital an extra two days as our newest love bug has spent some time wrapped up in a UV blanket like a glow worm. I also had some heavy spotting that was a bit worrying at first, so they just kept me here too.

"How's Lil No Name doing?" says Tess, peeking over the edge of my bed at the bundled baby.

I smile down at him, brushing a finger along his cheek. "Pink and perfect."

"Y'all goin' for three in three?"

"Hell no," I murmur, shifting back against my pillows. "The Price Pussy Palace is closed for renovations. You realize I've been pregnant for two years straight, right?"

"Of course, I do," she replies. "I ran out of creative mocktail ideas a year ago."

"God, I want a drink," I say with a sigh. "I wanna get trashed on shitty wine and dance in the kitchen knowing no one else inside my body is getting poisoned or jostled."

"We can make that happen," she replies. "Leave the babies with your boys, and you come over to my house for a rosé and sway party in my kitchen. We'll strip down to our undies and eat whipped cream straight from the can."

I laugh. "God, that sounds amazing."

"When do they get back?"

I tap my phone, lighting up the last text on my lock screen. "They're on the way."

As soon as Tess arrived, I made them all leave. They've been toughing it out for almost a week here at the hospital. But they needed showers and clean clothes, and I needed space. My hospital room looks like the aftermath of a slumber party with all the added chair and blankets, open duffle bags, empty drink bottles, and food containers.

Not to mention, my boys all shed socks like Tess sheds hair. Even now, I see one on the floor. God, who was in here taking his socks off? It's so unsanitary. I just shake my head with another tired sigh. I can't help but love them, socks on or off.

"Geez, your guys are slobs," Tess says, looking around.

"Only because they were distracted," I reply, which is mostly true. Ilmari in particular is a neat freak. But a bedridden wife and a sick baby has him all spun out right now. I'm sure he went home and feverishly cleaned while the others showered.

The socks thing though...that's been a staple argument in our house for three years. Jamie isn't even one yet, and even he adds to the mayhem. I find his cute little baby socks mixed in with theirs all over the place.

Tess gets up and starts to organize the room, shuffling the trash into the big can by the door. "Does No Name finally get a name today?"

I nod. "We should get the paternity test results back this afternoon."

The guys all agreed when I was pregnant with Jamie that the bio dad would get to name the baby. I came home from work one night to find them all sitting stoically at the kitchen table, the soft golden light casting shadows all around like something out of an oil painting. They were so

71

serious as they sat me down too. I swear, for a quick second there, I thought they were breaking up with me.

Instead, they walked me through their reasoning for letting the bio dad pick the baby's name. I was so relieved—and hormonal—that I broke down crying and Jake had to calm me down with ice cream while Cay rubbed my feet.

Before Tess can respond, there's a sharp tap at the door. My nurse comes in, heading to the sink to wash her hands. She's a lovely older black lady with kind eyes and a big smile. "Hey, mama. How's our boy doin?"

"Good," I say, shifting him a bit in my arms. "All he does is sleep."

"That's good. A well fed, sleepy baby is what we like to see. His tests all look great," she adds. "The jaundice has cleared beautifully. And you've been okayed too. Doc is ready to discharge you both."

"Yay," says Tess, coming around to sit in the chair again.

"And we have the paternity test results back," Nurse Kelly adds, her gaze locked on her tablet as she flicks and taps the screen.

Tess and I both go still, exchanging a glance.

"I...umm, well my guys aren't back yet," I say quickly. "I don't really want to know without them being here too."

"Ohmygod," Tess cries, digging her fingers into her curls. "I've been waiting nine months for this, Rachel! I can't wait any longer."

I slow turn to her, eyes narrowed. "You have a bet on this too, don't you?"

Her pouty pink lips open as she bats those lashes at me. "I—no—"

Yeah, she's a little liar. I'm sure the whole team has bets going. They did with Jamie too. If I wasn't so tired, I'd have the energy to be more annoyed.

At least everyone is acting in good faith. They're just excited to welcome the new baby. The Rays have been amazing. Sure, there were questions in the beginning. *Lots* of questions. The guys took most of that heat. But once we were all married and the deal was done, everyone settled. We're Team Price now, and no one who knows us bats an eye.

Tess huffs, arms crossed under her breasts. "Fine. Okay, yes. I'm in the pool, alright? I didn't win the due date bet. But I could still make a little money on the paternity results."

"How big is the pool?" I say, handing Lil No Name over to the nurse.

"You don't even wanna know," Tess replies.

Kelly just laughs. "We can wait til they get back, hon. It's no biggie."

"But you have it right there?" says Tess, peering over me. "Right on that little tablet, you've got the results? You could tell us?"

"Mhmm," Kelly replies, moving over to the corner to weigh and measure the baby.

"Leave her alone," I say at Tess.

"I can't believe you don't want to know," she huffs.

"I *do* want to know," I reply. "I just want to know with my guys here too. If they find out I found out, I'll never hear the end of it. Jake will pout for a month."

"God, and *nothing* is worth that," Tess grumbles.

Kelly laughs again, flashing a knowing smile as she shakes her head.

What can I say? Jake leaves an impression.

"Besides," I add. "I've waited this long. Another thirty minutes won't kill me."

A second nurse slips in and washes her hand before

going to help Kelly. The sound of fussing starts. No Name doesn't like being unswaddled from his cocoon. The moment I hear the first wail is the moment the door swings open and my guys all come back in.

Jake is in the lead looking washed and fresh, balancing a drink carrier with four coffees from our favorite local shop. Caleb shuffles in behind him, Jamie propped on his hip. Our firstborn is every inch his daddy, with Jake's dark hair and pretty green eyes.

"Nugget!" Tess squeals, hopping out of her chair to snatch him from Caleb's arms. She takes her godmother role very seriously, showering him with love and affection endlessly. We quickly had to put an embargo on toys though. Auntie Tess is now only allowed to express her love through experiences, not material goods. With exceptions for Christmas and birthdays, of course.

Ilmari comes in last, letting the door swing shut behind him.

Jake's bright smile falls as he hears the baby crying. His gaze darts from me to the corner. "What's wrong?"

"Nothing," I reply.

"He just didn't like getting his vitals checked," Kelly adds. She turns around with No Name bundled in her arms. "You're all going home today," she tells the guys.

"But the jaundice," says Jake.

"His bili count is great. He's good to go," she replies patiently.

"Oh, thank god." His shoulders slump with relief as he sets the coffees down on my hospital tray. "No offense, Kel. I mean, you've been a solid ten. But I wanna get the hell out of here."

She laughs again, handing the baby off to Ilmari.

I try to stop my lips from pursing in annoyance. I'm still

not used to his hair. He did it on a whim last week. One minute he was downstairs on the couch with us watching TV. The next, he disappeared and came down an hour later with his top knot gone. He'd shaved the whole thing off. He left a little hair on top, thank god. But his golden mane is in my trash can.

"I felt like a change," was all he said as we gaped at him.

He wanders around the end of the bed, baby in arms, and sits in the chair, humming and rocking to get No Name to settle. We're formula feeding him so the guys can all be more involved. As I watch, Jake gets a bottle ready. Meanwhile, Tess is bouncing Jamie on her hip by the window, blowing raspberries on his cheek to make him squeal and laugh.

Caleb takes the free moment to come around to the other side of my bed. "Hey, babe," he murmurs, his gaze not half so relaxed as his tone as he takes me in, kissing my forehead.

I take his hand, brushing my lips against his knuckles.

"Lunch is ready," Jake calls, holding up the bottle. "You or me, man?" he says at Ilmari.

"Me," Ilmari replies, reaching out his hand.

Jake stretches over the bed, passing him the bottle. Then he ducks down, kissing my lips. "Hey, gorgeous. You rest at all while we were gone?"

"Are you kidding?" I reply. "Tess was here."

"I heard that!" Tess calls.

"I got you a coffee," Jake laughs, handing me my cup. "And we can help you shower if you're up for it. Mars brought all the stuff you asked for."

I take the cup eagerly. It feels so warm against my palms. I lean my face over it, breathing deep. God, this scent is nirvana. I'm trying to give myself grace, but the feelings still creep in at least once a day. Am I monster for being *this* excited about not breastfeeding my own baby? Because I literally cannot wait to drown my liver in coffee and booze. It feels like I should be feeling sorry about that, but holding this coffee, it's hard to remember why.

"Tess, I didn't get you anything," Jake calls over his shoulder, snatching up his own coffee and handing one to Caleb. "Want Cay to go to Starbucks for you?"

Caleb punches his shoulder. "Volunteer yourself, asshole."

Tess and the nurses laugh. "I'm fine," she says. Then she glances over at me, biting her lip. "Actually...hey, uhh...what if I take my godson on a little trip down to the cafeteria? I'll just get a coffee down there."

All three of my guys go still as statues. Yeah, she's terrible at subterfuge. Her voice got all high and squeaky at the end.

"Oh shit," says Jake with a big grin. He spins around to face Kelly. "Are the results in?"

"The results are in," she replies.

"Okay, breathe everyone," he says, hand to his chest. In his crisp white t-shirt, black athletic shorts, and backwards Rays cap, he looks every inch my Sporty Ken doll.

"I'll just come back in a bit," says Tess, hitching Jamie up on her hip. The sound of his happy gurgling follows them out of the room.

Caleb slips around the end of the bed to snag the empty seat by Ilmari, peering over his shoulder as Ilmari feeds the baby.

"So, how y'all wanna do this?" says Kelly. "Want me to read it out for you? Want me to write it down, and y'all can read it out when I leave?"

"Just tell us," Jake begs as Caleb says, "Write it down."

She looks to me and I look wide-eyed back, my coffee raised halfway to my lips. "Well, I can't decide—"

"Babe, it has to be you," Jake urges.

"No way," I say, shaking my head. "Nope. I birthed these babies back to back. That was my job. I'm out. You're all deciding this."

"Write it down," calls Ilmari softly.

Jake sighs. "Fuck, that's two against one. Write it down, Kels."

With a smile, she shakes her head and pulls a pad of blue Post-its from her scrub pocket. She makes a show of turning around and using the wall to write on. Then she folds up the little Post-it and hands it out to Jake.

"What?" he squawks. "No way! I can't take it. God, are you kidding me?" He slinks away from her, ducking around the end of the bed to go sit on the arm of Caleb's chair.

"Well, someone has to take it," she teases, extending her arm.

All three of my guys lean away, like she's offering to let them pet a rattlesnake.

"God, just give it to me," I say, holding out my hand.

"You sure, mama?" she says, one dark brow raised.

"Yeah, hand it over. This way means I get to know first," I add, leveling a smirk at Jake.

"Hey, no fair," he cries.

"She literally just offered it to *you* first," Caleb reasons. "You could have read it to yourself and swallowed the paper. You could have kept us dangling for another hour. You chose to chicken out instead."

"Fuck," Jake mutters.

I sigh, handing the folded Post-it back to Kelly. "Just tell us."

"You sure?" she says again.

"Yeah," I reply. "We all know, or we all don't. Tell us, Kelly."

She glances over at the guys. A pregnant pause hangs in the air as we all wait. My heart is pounding. Not that this matters in the grandest scheme of things. My guys are all in three times over. Jamie may be Jake's biological son, but no one could love that baby more than Ilmari and Caleb. And they show their love every day. In that sense, bio dad status doesn't matter.

At the same time, I know just how much it matters. They can't help but be competitive. Protective. Possessive. They want to know, and I want them to know. It changes nothing collectively, even as it changes everything individually.

We all lean in, holding our breath.

Kelly's gaze settles on Ilmari and my tears start falling before she even speaks. "Mars is the father."

"Yes!" Jake whoops, hopping off the edge of Caleb's chair and punching the air. "God, I fucking *knew* it. Didn't I call it in the car on the way over here?" He hurries around the bed to wrap Kelly in a bear hug and kiss her cheek. She laughs, giving him a good natured shove.

I turn to the side to take in Ilmari and Caleb. Ilmari looks shocked, his massive hand rhythmically patting the baby's back. My gentle giant holding his son. My heart can't take it.

Caleb is smiling too, tears in his eyes. He leans over in his chair, one hand squeezing Ilmari's arm. "So happy for you, man."

I wipe under my eyes as Jake swoops forward to wrap me in a hug.

"I'll let you all be, and come back with the paperwork in a bit," says Kelly, heading for the door.

"Thanks, Kel!" Jake calls. Then he rattles down the side

of my bed and climbs in with me, squishing me with his weight, but I don't mind. He slings a leg over me, nestling his face in at my neck.

I feel tired and unwashed. I'm still wearing those mesh underwear things with the witch hazel cooling pads on my battered vaj. But none of that matters now. Jake certainly doesn't care.

"Babe, you are so fucking amazing," he murmurs, nuzzling me and kissing up my jaw. "You make us the most beautiful babies."

Tears sting my eyes again as I look at little No Name in his daddy's arms.

"We're so goddamn lucky. You know that, right?" Jake adds, his hand brushing my shoulder. "You have us, and we have you, and we have two beautiful, healthy babies. We're so lucky, guys."

Caleb nods, his eyes still locked on Ilmari and the baby. "He needs a name," he says. "It's time."

Ilmari goes still, his gaze unfocused as he holds the baby closer to him. No Name is quiet, already happily asleep again in Ilmari's arms.

"Mars never wanted to play the name game," says Jake. "I had like a thousand good ideas if Glow Worm was mine. I know Cay had one or two. But I could never squeeze any names out of you."

"It felt like tempting fate," Ilmari replies.

"Well, bio dad names the baby. That's you, champ," Jake says, kissing my shoulder. He's careful of my IVs, ghosting over them to pick up my hand, massaging it. "I just did a mash-up of mine and Amy's names. Jake and Amy became Jamie. Boom. Done."

I smile, taking another sip of my coffee with my free hand.

"Yeah, but Mars doesn't have any siblings to do a mash-up like that," Caleb reasons.

"He can just combine his name with Rachel's," Jake replies with a shrug. "Like...Ilchel."

"Ramari," Caleb teases.

"Ilra," Jake adds with a laugh.

"Shut up, and let him think," I say.

"Ooo, let's stick with the gods thing," Jake says, ignoring me. "We'll have Mars and his son Jupiter. Or—who's the other god of war, Cay? Mars is Gree..." He drags out the sound with a raised brow.

"Roman," Caleb and Ilmari correct at the same time.

"Right. So who's the Greek one?"

"Ares," Caleb supplies.

"Ohmygod," Jake gasps, sitting up and nearly spilling my coffee. "How freaking perfect is that? Mars is an Ares and his son is named Ares!"

"Nah, it's two different spellings," Caleb corrects, sipping his coffee. "Aries and Ares."

"Yeah, but no one would know unless it's written down," Jake shrugs.

"That's just confusing," Cay replies.

Jake leans over me. "Hey Mars, who's the god of war in Finnish mythology?"

"Iku-Turso," he replies, not looking up. "Or sometimes he is called Tursas."

Caleb holds back a cringe, glancing at me. "I mean, I know we're not voting here, and there's no veto option...but I would veto Iku-Turso."

"Same," I reply.

"I still think we were onto something with the whole gods thing," Jake goes on. "We've already got a Mars and a Poseidon. What about Thor?"

"Thor is Norse," Ilmari replies.

"Yeah, so?" Jake says with a shrug.

Ilmari stares at him. "I'm Finnish."

"Well, then I'm out of ideas," Jake says with a shrug.

"Thank god," I reply with a teasing smile.

While Jake huffs at me, Ilmari shifts the baby off his shoulder, cradling him in one arm. He lifts his free hand, brushing a finger feather-light along his sleeping son's brow. "Tuomas," he says softly.

"What?" I say.

"His name is Tuomas," Ilmari replies. "Tuomas Caleb Price."

"Thomas?" Jake repeats.

"The Finnish way," Ilmari corrects. "Tuomas."

"It's beautiful," I say. "Why Tuomas?"

Ilmari shrugs, his eyes still on his baby. "I had no father figure in my young life. I had hockey and I had music. Tuomas Holopainen is the lead songwriter for Nightwish, one of my favorite bands. I listened to their music in the gym, on the road. I never had a father giving me confidence before a game. I had Tuomas Holopainen."

"I love it," Jake says. "Really, Mars. It's perfect. Is Nightwish some of your heavy metal stuff?"

Ilmari nods.

Jake grins. "That is so rock n' roll. Grandpa Hal is gonna flip. Our little Tuomas the rocker. And Glow Worm still makes a cool nickname," he adds, kissing my brow.

"Why Caleb?" I say, glancing over to Cay. He's still yet to say a word or make an outward reaction to our son's new name.

Ilmari sighs and looks to Caleb. A long moment stretches between them where he doesn't say anything.

"Jake makes me happy," he says at last. "Rachel makes me feel whole," he adds. "But you make me feel safe."

Caleb sucks in a breath, leaning away.

Tears sting my eyes as I watch them. Next to me, Jake is utterly still.

"You know...you've never said it to me before," Ilmari murmurs. There's a vulnerability in his voice that I don't know I've ever heard before. "It's been almost four years, and you've never said it," he says with a shake of his head. Tears rim his blue eyes.

"Mars," says Caleb, mirroring his head shake.

"I feel it every day," Ilmari goes on, glancing down at the baby. "I see it. I know it to be true. But...will you say it now?" He looks up, holding Caleb's gaze again. "Will you take this son I name for you, and say it?" He leans forward, holding the baby out to Caleb.

A silent tear slips down my cheek as I watch them.

"Please," Ilmari murmurs.

Hearing that word, Caleb breaks, his own tears falling. He leans forward in his chair over the baby, gripping Ilmari's bearded face with both hands. "Of course, I'll fucking say it." Then he's kissing Ilmari's temple, his forehead. "I love you, Mars. Fuck, I love you so much. I love you. I'll tell you every fucking day."

Ilmari breaks too, one protective hand holding Tuomas close as he reaches out with his free hand, fisting the front of Caleb's shirt, burying his face at Caleb's shoulder.

It's only in hearing it now that I realize it's true. I tell Ilmari I love him every day. Multiple times a day. And Jake has never been stingy with his affection. He hugs Ilmari all the time. He'll snuggle him on the couch, saying he needs his Finny Bear. Jake's the best at Christmases and birthdays, making everyone feel special and loved.

I always knew Caleb was the most reserved with words of affirmation. I've grown to accept it seeing how well he proves himself with action. But I at least have heard the words. I can't imagine being in Ilmari's position, never hearing them uttered.

I cling to Jake, watching Ilmari and Caleb break apart. Ilmari keeps ahold of his shirt and Caleb keeps his hand on Ilmari's shoulder.

"Will you love our son?" Ilmari asks. "Will you keep him safe as you keep me safe?"

Caleb nods, one hand dropping down to cup his son's head. "I will." He leans down, kissing his brow. "I'm gonna love you so much, little guy. You and your daddies. Your mom. Your beautiful brother."

He glances up, looking at me. The depths of his dark eyes are bottomless as he pulls me in. Ilmari's soft confession has shattered his walls to dust. "I love you, Hurricane. So fucking much. You made me a father, a husband. You're the reason I have any of this," he adds, gesturing around the room. "You make Mars feel whole, but you make me feel seen. You see me, baby. And I pray to god you *never* look away."

I shake my head. "Never," I reply. "Cay baby, never."

He closes his eyes, taking a deep breath, his hands still on Ilmari and Tuomas.

Next to me, Jake shifts, wiping his eyes. "Well, Mars feels whole and Cay feels seen, but you set me free, Seattle." He tucks the loose strands of dark hair back behind my ear. "Meeting you in that bar is the best thing that ever happened to me. I'm free now. Free to love, free to live. You're amazing, Rachel Price. You're a gift." He kisses my brow and we breathe each other in. I know he feels the same as I do, his mere presence enough to spin me up, even as he calms me down.

Ilmari gets out of his chair and Jake takes my coffee so he can place the baby in my arms. With his hands free, Ilmari cups my face and kisses me. "Mä rakastan sua."

"Niin mäkin sua," I whisper against his lips.

"You know, you've never said it to me in Finnish before," Jake teases, looking up at Ilmari.

Ilmari stills. Then he leans over me, cupping Jake's neck to kiss his forehead. "Mä rakastan sua, Jake."

Jake smiles bright, one hand on his chest. "Okay, I legit just felt a heart flutter. Why was that so hot?"

Ilmari and I both laugh as he leans away. "I'm already married."

"Love you too, Mars," Jake replies.

Ilmari steps back to let Caleb in.

Caleb looks at the baby in my arms before giving me a kiss. "More than my own life," he intones. "All of you. The five of you. I love you more than my own life."

I nod, shifting my hold on the baby to cup Caleb's stubbled cheek. A curl of his reddish brown hair falls over his brow. "You're mine, Cay. You're *ours*. These babies. This family. We need you. Love us and let us love you."

Caleb heaves a grateful sigh as he nods, his shoulders relaxing.

Ilmari steps in beside him.

Next to me, Jake sits up, setting his coffee aside. "I don't know about you guys, but I'm ready to get the fuck outta here. Why don't we go track down Kelly, let Mars sign the birth certificate, and we all go home?"

I smile as the other two groan with relief.

"I'll go hunt down Tess and J-man," says Caleb, heading for the door.

"And I'll go find Kelly," says Jake, slipping off the bed to follow him.

"And you're going to take this," I say at Ilmari, gesturing to the baby.

He raises his brow. "What? No, I'm going to pack your things and make you ready."

"No, you're gonna take this baby," I reply. "Like, *now* Ilmari. Take him from my arms. Now."

At my urgent tone, he doesn't hesitate, reaching out for the baby. "Why, what's wrong? Are you unwell?"

"No," I reply, flinging back the thin hospital sheets to expose my unshaved legs poking out the bottom of my unflattering hospital gown.

Ilmari shifts the baby to one arm, reaching for me. "Rakas, what—"

"Jeez, nothing's wrong," I laugh, shuffling forward in my ugly red hospital socks. "I just *really* have to pee."

6

KING OF THE ICE

"Daddy!" Jamie squirms in my arms, trying to get closer to the glass as Jake flashes by in a blur of teal.

"Yeah, bubs. That's daddy," I say pointing him out.

As we watch, Jake slams a Capitals forward into the corner, fighting to clear the puck out of the Rays defense zone.

"Daddy bang!" Jamie squeals, drawing laughter from the fans around us.

The crowd goes wild as the Rays defend their zone. Meanwhile, Jamie is losing interest fast. After two periods of good behavior, he's a wiggly eel in my arms, desperate to get down and run. But I can't chase him right now. I can't think about anything except what's happening out on that ice. If we can hold on for eight more minutes, we're going to win this game and clinch a playoffs position. The Rays could win their first Stanley Cup.

"Down," Jamie whines. "Dada—want down."

"No, bubs. No down," I say distractedly, holding him closer as he squirms.

Next to me, Mars has it easy. Tuo is like a baby koala. So

long as he's being held, he's happy. He's tucked inside his baby backpack, sporting a Rays beanie and noise cancelling headphones, his pacifier bobbing as he just looks around, happy to be included.

I groan as Jamie kicks.

"Down, Dada—"

"Get it out!"

"Fight!"

"Come on, Rays!"

All around us, the crowd is howling as Jake gets into another corner battle. Our newly traded goalie is on high alert, crouched low, watching the action. Jake wins control, slapping the puck out across the ice. Langley turns with it on a dime, blasting down the rink. Jake recovers, skating up to his spot on the red line, guarding the zone with Novy.

"He's playing well," Ilmari says at my side.

I follow his gaze and smirk. Of course he's watching the new guy, not *our* guy. No. 1, Hunter DeGraw. This is only his third game starting with the Rays. He's young, only twenty-three, snatched from an LA Kings farm team on a clever trade by our GM. He's just as tall as Mars, broad-shouldered, and possibly even faster (though I'd never say that out loud). The problem is he drifts left. He's let in two goals tonight, both on the right side.

Thank god our forwards are on fire and made three of their own goals to make up the difference. Jake even had an assist on the last one. Karlsson put it right between the goalie's legs. DeGraw's been playing better this period, over-correcting to show the Capitals he can guard his right side too.

"We'll win," says Mars with total confidence.

"Don't jinx us," I mutter, my gaze locked on the far end

of the rink where our forwards are fighting to get the puck in the net.

"We'll win," Mars says again.

"Isä win?" Jamie says, tugging on my Rays hat and flipping it off my head.

Mars catches it with his quick reflexes, handing it back to me.

"Isä, want down," Jamie whines, reaching for Mars. "Tuo, down too." He leans over, trying to reach his little brother. "Tuo, down?"

Tuomas drops his pacifier and babbles at his brother in baby talk, reaching out a chubby hand. Ilmari leans in, saying something in quick Finnish, kissing Jamie's cheek and tapping a finger to the tip of his nose.

Jamie whines again, slinging himself around in my arms like a thrashing shark. For only being three years old, he's so damn strong. I blame Jake and his Minnesota mountain man genes. "Ouch, *fuck*—" I grunt as Jamie's swinging foot collides with my dick.

"Fuck! Daddy fuck, fuck," Jamie parrots.

I groan as Ilmari gives me fierce side eye. He doesn't need to say anything. I know I'm adding a dollar to the swear jar. At this point, they should just rename the damn thing the 'Caleb Jar.' It's not fair though because Mars swears in Finnish all the time and we just don't know so it doesn't count. Stupid double standards.

"Unintentional," I mutter, shifting Jamie over to my other hip, taking careful hold of his swinging foot.

"Down!" he squawks louder. His little cheeks grow redder as he gets frustrated at being denied.

"Bubs, there's only five more minutes," I plead, trying to keep my focus on both the game and my squirrelly kid.

"Here," says Mars. "Unbuckle me." He turns to the side, showing me his back.

I reach up on reflex, eyes locked on the game, and unbuckle the strap securing the baby carrier.

Mars makes quick work of lifting Tuo out. "Switch."

The crowd around us cheers while we trade kids. Mars tucks a squirming, angry Jamie into the front of the carrier, leaving me to hold a happy Tuo. Baby bubs gazes up at me, his little hands holding to my chin as I watch DeGraw make an awesome stick save.

"Yes!" Ilmari shouts, holding down Jamie's slappy hands. "Glove! Glove!"

DeGraw scrambles after the rebound, flopping on his stomach on the ice and diving for the puck, closing his glove down around it to stop play.

"Yes!" we both shout.

My gaze shoots across the ice to the Rays bench. Rachel is working tonight. She's standing sentry in the corner, arms crossed, watching the action. Jerry stands at her side, leaning over to say something that has her laughing.

Fuck, why did I switch shifts with him tonight? I could be right in the action too. I could be there to congratulate Jake when he steps off that ice, knowing he's leading the Rays into their first playoffs. That's the last time I do Jerry a favor to cover his damn dentist appointment.

Jake takes up his position at the face-off circle, waiting for the puck to drop. The large captain's "C" is stitched proudly on his chest. My best friend, my husband, starting defenseman and captain of an NHL team. It still doesn't feel real sometimes. My wife works the bench while my husband skates...oh, and my *other* husband stands at my side soothing one of my babies.

How did I get so fucking lucky? I'm the most undeserving of assholes, blessed to have things I didn't even know I wanted.

I glance down at Tuo's face, soaking in those pink cheeks and dark blue eyes. Under the hat, he's got a head of almond brown curls, the perfect mix of Rachel and Mars. My sweet boy. Feeling overwhelmed, I lean down and kiss his brow. He sucks that pacifier, fisting my Rays t-shirt with both hands.

Ilmari's bouncing and swaying has soothed Jamie. Poor little guy is just as tired as he is excited. His bedtime was an hour ago. I watch his head sink down onto Ilmari's chest as his eyes begin to droop. Being strapped in the carrier is calming him down. I envy my boys their ability to sleep anywhere, even front row at an NHL hockey game.

The minutes are ticking down in this final period. Only four left. DeGraw slaps the puck hard with his paddle, sending it flying up the ice. Langley all but stumbles to chase after it. The Capitals defense send it back over our line, aiming for a forward, but it lands right on the end of Jake's stick instead. He fakes left, then he's blasting forward, taking the puck over the line towards the Capitals goal.

"Go! Go!"

"Priiiiice!"

Everyone around us is yelling.

"Pass it," I shout. "Karlsson's open!"

"No, he's not," Mars calls at my side. And he's right. The Capitals forward has caught up to Karlsson, cutting him off. Karlsson gets checked back.

"Keep it!"

"Shoot it!"

"Fake him out!"

All my air is trapped in my throat as everyone around me suddenly becomes an expert in stick and puck handling.

But nothing we say matters. Only what Jake sees, what he feels. If it's right, he'll take the shot. If not, he'll fall back and regroup.

Mars steps in close, his arm wrapping around my waist as we both hold our breath. "Take the shot," he murmurs only loud enough for me to hear.

It's just Jake and the goalie now. Every other Capitals player is getting effectively boxed out by a Ray.

Now or never.

"Come on, take the shot," I whisper, willing Jake to hear me.

My voice is lost to the roar of the crowd as Jake slashes left, luring the goalie with him, only to do another fancy flick with his stick, sinking the puck into the back corner of the net. The lights go off, the bullhorn blasts, and Bruno Mars fills the Rays stadium as Jake gets hammered on all sides by celebrating Rays.

The Rays are now winning 4-2. The fans around us scream. Those closest know who we are, so we get our shoulders squeezed and patted. A bearded man with Bud Light breath puffs in my face, "Your guy is fuckin' awesome!"

"Best defense is a good offense," his equally drunk friend shouts.

I smile but put a protective hand around Tuo, inching closer to Mars. We do our best to thank everyone and the cheering intensifies as Jake comes skating down the ice. He knows where we are. He made faces at the boys through the glass during warmups.

Rays fans slam the glass as Jake skates up, trailed by Novy. He's smiling wide, his bright blue mouthguard hanging out the side of his mouth, clenched in his teeth. I glance over and see Jamie is zonked out against Ilmari's chest, his breathing deep and even.

Tuomas pops his pacifier out of his mouth. "Da—da—" he babbles, reaching out both hands towards Jake.

"Did you see that shot?" Jake teases at me. "You couldn't have done it any prettier."

I just smirk, leaning forward to let Tuo put his hands on the glass.

Distracted by the baby, Jake taps the glass with his gloved finger. "Did you see me, Tuo? Did you see Daddy's goal?"

The whistle blows and Jake turns, popping his mouth-guard back in. This game is over. The Rays are advancing to the playoffs. But there's still three minutes left in this game.

"Tell DeGraw he played well," Ilmari calls, both his large hands resting protectively over Jamie's back.

Glancing back at us, Jake nods. He tears his gaze from the babies, focusing all his heated attention on me. A moment that lasts endless seconds stretches between us as he holds my gaze. Then he gives me a wink and skates off.

Fuck me dead.

My heart stops as my dick twitches. I watch him skate into position, ready for the puck drop. Once he's bent over, stick in position, he glances my way again with a teasing grin, flashing me that blue mouth guard.

"Fuck," I mutter, shifting on my feet.

"Fu, fu, fu," Tuo echoes, tapping my stubbled chin with both his tiny hands.

"*Ouch*—" I wince as Ilmari elbows me. *Hard.*

"I'm going to raise the swear jar price to one hundred dollars per swear," he warns.

"You have to admit, I'm getting better," I say with a shrug, elbowing him back.

He just rolls his eyes, his attention on the puck drop.

The players all know they're running out the clock. No

way the Capitals are coming back from this in under two minutes. The forwards are still fighting, but Jake easily bats the puck loose and sends it flying down the rink.

Taking his cue from Novy, they dart for the side and hop over the boards. Morrow and J-Lo take their place on the ice. Jake is done for this game. The others on the bench are already congratulating him, including Hurricane. She leans over him, both hands on his shoulders, kissing the side of his helmet, her smile wide.

Fuck, I want him. I feel suddenly breathless as the need crashes over me, buffeting me like a wave. Watching him skate is hot enough. But watching him win? Watching him dominate? It has the demon deep inside me breathing fire, desperate to show him how well he can be dominated too.

It's been weeks since I've had him all to myself. They says kids change things, and they weren't lying. Between all the crazy schedules and the travel, I'm struggling to remember the last time I had my way with him alone. Why can't I picture it? The shower, I think. He'd just come home from an away game.

That flirty wink replays in my mind easily enough—the curve of his smile, the sweat on his brow. He's all confidence tonight, all power and control. I need him to cede it to me. Need him to remind us both who we are and what we crave.

And I crave that man like I crave air.

My husband. My lover. My fucking soul mate.

Well...one of them.

I groan again, watching the clock tick down.

"What's wrong with you?" Ilmari mutters, nudging me.

I shift my hold on Tuomas. "Nothing. I'm fine." My gaze is still locked on Jake across the ice. He's standing now, gloves and helmet off, clapping and cheering for the team, his smile making my chest feet tight.

Next to me, Ilmari snorts and shakes his head. "Seriously?"

I glare at him. "What?"

He holds my gaze. "You think I don't know you? You think I don't know that look?" he adds, pointing at my face with a smirk.

"Shut up," I mutter.

He huffs a soft laugh. After a minute, he reaches out. "Give him to me."

I pull back. "What? No, I—"

"Just give him to me," he says again, lifting Tuomas away and holding both boys at once.

"Mars—"

"If you get caught, I had nothing to do with it," he mutters.

"You're a terrible influence, you know," I tease. "And this is way worse than a little swearing. You're about to be complicit in a crime."

He raises a brow at me. "Are you planning to rob a concession stand?"

"More like defile one," I reply.

He just laughs. "Go, before I change my mind. And before the crowds swarm," he adds, gesturing up at the ticking game clock.

Shit, I have less than two minutes. People are already starting to flood out while most of the stadium celebrates.

"You got the babies?" I say, letting myself feel a slight twinge of guilt before Ilmari is elbowing me.

"*Go.*"

I take off up the stairs, keeping my head down in case any fans try to snag my attention. I know this stadium like the back of my hand, and I've got my security pass in my pocket. Mars had to turn his in when he retired, so he technically can't get down to the locker room without an escort. But the guards all know him and they all love Rachel. When they see him sporting double babies, they'll let him right through.

The final game buzzer sounds and the crowd roars as I duck down a stairwell, flashing my pass to get into the tunnels. Once there, I'm able to avoid the crowds, weaving my way around the rink and over towards the locker room.

"Hey, Mr. Price! Great game," calls a friendly security guard.

I jog past him with a wave, ignoring the twinge in my knee. Between Hurricane's strength and conditioning regiment and Jake's massages, I've seen drastic improvement in my range of motion, even if the pain still flares, especially after a long day like today. Right now, I hardly notice it. I'm a man on a mission.

I know I've got some time yet. The press will hold Jake back for an on-ice interview. As captain, they'll want to hear from him his thoughts on the game and our playoff prospects. The man is a PR dream—handsome, well spoken, charming as sin. He could sell a bag of dildos to a nun.

Fuck, that smirk he gave me out on the ice. He lobbed it like a grenade, right over the plexiglass. *Boom.* If he thinks he can play with my fire, I'm gonna remind him what it feels like to get burned. Goddamn, I need him bad. I take a breath, trying to cool the heat in my blood. I can't wander around the tunnels sporting a tent in my pants. This is my place of business, after all.

Get it together, asshole.

There's a hitch in my step as I smirk. Seeing as I'm literally on a mission to track down my husband and pound him senseless, I'm not the poster child for ethical workplace professionalism right now.

I laugh, shaking my head. Yeah, I don't give a fuck. Daddy Cay is done wrangling pacifiers and holding babies tonight. My big time NHL superstar is gonna drop to his knees and make me feel like a whole other kind of daddy.

I round the corner at the long end of the main tunnel, my mind spinning out the possibilities of where. The caveman in me wants to put him on his knees in the middle of the damn locker room. But voyeurism isn't his kink unless Rachel and Mars are the ones watching.

He *does* have a serious kink for almost getting caught, which could be fun. Private sex in public. Yeah, my good boy goes weak for a handy on the plane. And he's all for indulging mine and Rachel's love of gritty bar bathrooms. We almost got kicked out of a karaoke bar down at Jax Beach when we fucked so hard we broke the sink. Water sprayed everywhere. We came out soaking wet wearing shit-eating grins.

But I don't want to exchange handys up against the stall of a bathroom, hands over our mouths to stifle our groans. I want to throw him around a little. I want to hear him moan, watch him beg.

There's only one place in mind. *Our* place. At this point we should just go all in and get a plaque for the door. The Price Family Storage Closet. It's far enough from the locker room that we don't have to be too quiet. And there's room for all four of us inside. Fuck, we've had some fun in that damn closet.

"Hey Sanny!" Morrow calls with a wave. "What a fuckin' game, eh?"

I smile at him. "Well played."

"Did you see your boy out there? Cap was on fire

tonight," says Fields from behind him. They're still in their gear, handing their gloves and sticks off to the waiting EMs.

"You're off the clock tonight, eh boss?" calls Cody, one of the new hires. He catches a pair of gloves as Karlsson tosses them to him, and pops them on the rack.

"Yep," I say. "Scuse me, gentlemen."

I slip right past them, moving towards the locker room. I go to turn the corner just as Rachel comes hopping out.

"Oh—hey, babe." She pops up on her toes to give me a quick kiss. She looks tired but wired, her bun a little frizzy and her eye makeup smudged. But she's in her element. "Playoffs here we come," she adds. "Have you seen Jake yet?"

"No—"

"God, he's gonna be insufferable for a week," she says with a laugh. "He's already threatening me that I have to call him 'King of the Ice.'" She grabs my arm as I try to slip past her. "Hey—you okay, baby?"

I suck in a breath, giving her my full attention. "Yeah."

Her gorgeous dark eyes dart left then right, her expression concerned as she reads me like no one else has ever been able to do. Mars comes close. Then she's smiling through pursed lips, shaking her head. "Ohh...yeah you're just fine, aren't you," she teases. "I'd join you, but I've got my hands full here for another hour," she adds, gesturing to the plastic box slung under one arm stocked with ice bags and wraps.

"He in there?" I say, gesturing with a nod to the locker room.

"Yeah. Just finished press. Hey—go gentle with him," she adds. "Pepper in a little praise. He needs it."

With that, my wife kisses my cheek and saunters off, perfectly comfortable in the knowledge that I'm planning to go corner and fuck our husband. Yeah, that woman was made for me. I'll remind her why tonight.

But right now is all about Jake. Mr. King of the Ice.

I slip into the locker room to find the guys in various states of undress. The funk in this room post game is something not for the faint of heart as all the layers of sweaty gear get stripped off and tossed in the big laundry bin. After twenty years in the life, I'm used to it.

"Sanny!"

"Sanford!"

"It's Price now, dickhead," Novy growls, shoving Walsh.

"Ouch—*shit*—Why is Sanny okay, but not Sanford?"

"Because it is," Novy snaps.

I just shake my head. I'll leave it to Novy to put the third string guy in his place. When we all changed our names, the guys faced a brief conundrum of what to do having four Prices on the team. Rachel became 'Doc' and for the short time Mars was still playing, he was just Mars. The guys all just stuck with 'Sanny' for me. Only Jake's name really changed. No one calls him 'Compton' anymore. It's only ever—

"Price!" Coach Johnson shouts from the other doorway. "He in here?"

"Showers, sir," DeGraw calls back. He has Ilmari's stall now, which means he gears up next to Jake for every game.

Coach looks around for one of the assistant captains. "J-Lo, with me," he calls, turning and ducking back out.

J-Lo shuffles off, still in his skates.

I step fully into the locker room, moving over towards DeGraw. He's a handsome guy. Young and fit. Unattached. The Jacksonville bunny network went crazy with his trade. But he doesn't seem into that life. He's a bit of a closed book all the way around, really.

"Hey," I say at him. "Ilmari watched your game."

He perks up immediately. Ilmari Price is akin to a living god in the hockey goalie world. "Yeah?"

"Yeah. You played good. You're watching your right side better. He noticed."

He flashes me a smile, giving a relieved nod. "Hey, thanks, bud."

I nod and slip past him, ducking into the showers. It takes me no time to see Jake isn't there, so I slip into the connecting changing room where the guys keep their warmup gear and street clothes.

I hear him before I see him. It's his magnetic laugh. It hooks me deep in my chest and reels me in. I can't not follow that laugh. I need to see him. Need to feel him. I won't be able to breathe until he's in my arms.

I step in the doorway to see Jake standing in the corner, his dark hair sticking up all over like he just roughed it with a towel. His toned ass flexes as he tugs a pair of grey boxer briefs up his wet legs.

"Hey, Sanny," Langley calls, pulling on his shirt. "Did you see our captain out there tonight?"

"Playoffs, baby!

"Stanley, here we come!"

The other guys hoot and shove each other, still cele-brating their win. But I only care about one guy. *My* guy. Jake turns, glancing over his shoulder at me, smile still on his face. I cross my arms, leaning against the doorjamb and level my gaze at him, heart pounding. Fuck, he's so goddamn beautiful. How did I go nearly ten years surviving on our "just friends" bullshit?

"Where are the babies?" he calls over at me. He peers down, as if he expects to see Jamie dart around the open door. Our kids are a feature of the home games. This arena and the practice facility are practically their second homes.

"With Mars," I say.

"How bout that last goal, eh?" says Perry. "I think Cap is gunning for a forward position."

"Yeah, and you'll be the first one benched," Langley teases, throwing his wet towel at him.

Perry catches it, dropping it to the floor.

I haven't taken my eyes off Jake. I tell him everything I'm feeling. Everything I need. Let's see how well he's listening. Because if he doesn't take the hint and come to me in the next sixty seconds, I'll be making this private moment real fucking public. I'm about to scar his teammates for life.

Come on, angel.

Jake smirks, giving me a little half shoulder shrug as if to say, "What's your problem?"

I wait.

We hold eye contact a second longer and I give him everything, letting this burning feeling coiling in my chest burst outward.

Fucking come here to me. Crawl. Beg. Now.

His cheeks bloom pink as he looks quickly away and I smile.

Got him.

Snatching for his shorts and shirt, he tugs them on. I don't wait. Spinning on my heel, I duck out of the changing room, using the door that leads out into the hallway. I turn sharply left and start walking down the hall towards the storage room.

"Hey," Jake calls, ducking out of the changing room. "You okay? Babe, where you goin'? How 'bout that goal, huh?" His Nike slides slap on the concrete as he jogs to catch up. "I think I make a pretty good forward. Cay—hey—"

I let him keep talking as I take a sharp left, turning down the narrow hall that leads to the Price Family Storage Closet.

"Cay—"

As soon as he clears the corner, I turn, grabbing him by the shirt and shoving him up against the wall. He grunts as I pin him in place with my hips. Then I cup his stubbled cheeks with both hands and take what I need, kissing him senseless.

"Fuck—" He pants against my mouth, his confusion spiraling quickly into arousal as our cocks harden, locked together by the press of my hips.

We're both wearing nothing but athletic gear so there's no hiding the way we make the other feel. His hands quickly come up to grip my elbows, then he drops them down to cup my ass, cursing against my lips as he pulls me even tighter against him. We both groan, chasing each kiss with tongues and teeth.

His kisses are playful and passionate, proof that he's here. He's with me. His brain is always spinning a million miles a minute, but sex is one of the only things proven to focus him to a single task. *Pleasure.* My Jake goes all in every time. He's present, he's adoring. He pays attention. I fucking love that about him.

"Cay—" He breaks our kiss, his hands sliding up to brace my hips. His pretty green eyes blink at me, dark with arousal. "What—"

"I need you," I admit, my thumb brushing down the column of his throat, over his Adam's apple.

"What do you need?" he murmurs, his gaze locked on me. That's another thing I love about him. He *looks* at people. He sees them. He makes them feel seen. Rachel and Mars do it too. I feel inexplicably, blessedly *seen* by my family.

"You."

He nods, his hands trailing up to curl around my wrists. My hands still cup his face. He leans in, brushing his lips against mine. It's not a kiss. We're just connecting, getting in sync. "What do you need, baby?"

I go stiff, my breath caught in my chest. Normally it doesn't bother me when Jake and Hurricane call me 'baby.' It's just a term of endearment. We all have them for each other. And the kids each have a list of them a mile long. But in this moment, with my heart beating fast, blood pumping to my dick...yeah, I'm no one's baby right now.

His lips part on a breath as his eyes darken. "Oh." Then he pecks my mouth once more, running his hands down my chest. "Fucking finally. It's been ages since you've come out to play." Dropping his hand down, he gives my dick a squeeze.

I groan.

"You have lube?" he says, leaning in to kiss my neck, my ear. His scent surrounds me. "I can't say I've prepped for a hard pounding. But if you're offering, I'm saying yes. Hell yes. You have lube, Cay?"

I grip the back of his neck, pulling him back to hold his gaze. "Do I look like a fucking amateur?"

His smile widens as he strokes my dick again. "Then what are you waiting for, daddy? Tear this ass apart."

I growl, shoving him back. "Get in the fucking closet."

His chest heaves, eyes bright with excitement as he follows my order, slipping in his sandals as he races to pull the utility closet door open. I'm right behind him, snapping it shut and turning the lock.

It's less a closet and more of a small warehouse-style room. With tall ceilings and shelves along two walls, it's cluttered with everything from cleaning supplies to overflow gear piles. Our favorite feature is the old collection of goalie nets stacked in the corner.

Yeah, Mars has a major net kink, which might be a kink specific to hockey goalies. He loves fucking our girl against them. He's usually the last to agree to public sex, which is why this closet is so much fun for all of us. If he even thinks we'll have fun with her against a net without him, he's the first to whip out his dick.

Jake spins around, standing in the middle of the space in his Rays t-shirt, navy blue shorts, and athletic socks. He's my bi hockey sex dream. Fuck, I love him so goddamn much. Crossing the space between us, I grab him and shove him towards the nearest supply shelf.

"Shit," he pants, his back rattling against the shelf. The whole unit squeaks as, behind his head, the rows of purple Shine Wow surface cleaner jiggle. He grins, hands going to my hips. "Damn, baby. You need it that rough?"

"I'm not your goddamn baby," I say, my hand going to his throat.

He whimpers at the contact, arching his neck. He's as bad as Rachel. They both love a good choking. "Tell me what to do," he says, his tone breathless. "Tell me what you need."

I sink into dom space, taking deep breaths as I let my hand constrict around his throat. I can't offer him the praise I know he craves until I'm allowed a little degradation first. "So you were the big man tonight, huh?" I tease. "You're out there making plays? King of the fucking ice, right? A goal and an assist. You must feel like a god right now."

He smirks. He can't help but brat, even if we both know he'll fold like a house of cards in sixty seconds. Rachel is the true switch of the family. No one can domme from her knees like our queen.

"You saw me out there," he replies, his voice hoarse from my fist squeezing him tight. "Did I look like a king to you? That's *my* fucking ice."

I lean in, my hand tightening at his throat as I use the other to jerk his shorts down around his ankles. "You can be a king out on the ice. But who are you in here?" I growl, fisting his dick.

He groans, eyes fluttering shut. "Yours."

"Try again," I say, jerking him dry. The friction has us both panting. "Are you a king in here, angel?"

He shakes his head, his hands gripping the shelf as he tries to sink into the sensation of me stroking him.

"Speak," I snap.

"*Ahh*—no," he pants. "You're the king. You're the god. You're the emperor of the fucking universe, just don't fucking stop."

"And who are you?" I say, nipping his jaw before I'm sucking his throat. I swipe my thumb over his tip, taking that precum and getting him slick.

"Fuck," he whimpers, his hands leaving the shelves to grip my hips.

"Did I say you could touch me?" I snap, my hand stilling on his dick.

With a groan, he raises both hands, holding the shelf that rests behind his head. "Take me," he pleads. "Use me. I'm your dirty fucking whore. Please, Cay—"

I silence him with a kiss, dropping my hand from his throat to free myself from my athletic pants. But not before I tug loose my wallet, keys, and phone from my pocket, rattling them down on the shelf behind him. "Take off your shirt."

Jake rushes to comply, stripping himself naked for me. He drops the Rays t-shirt to our feet, his cut muscles looking so defined after a night of athleticism out on that ice.

Ducking down, I kiss his chest, teasing his nipple between my teeth.

"Oh god," he groans, knocking my hat off so he can fist my hair.

"Get the lube," I say. "Wallet."

He groans, fumbling as I trail my tongue across his chest, teasing his other nipple into a dark brown peak. Between us, his cock bobs, desperate for some attention.

"There's two," he pants, finding the individual packets of lube tucked into my wallet. Did I plan to fuck my husband in a closet tonight? You can't always plan for these things. Best to be prepared.

"One now," I reply. "You're gonna fist our cocks. Get me ready to take that ass."

He sighs with relief as he tears open the first lube packet. Squeezing it into his hand, he's careful as he drops it down, wrapping our dicks together in his fist. "Of—fuck me —fuck—"

We both look down, foreheads pressed together as we watch him coat our dicks with lube. It feels fucking amazing. His dick against mine, the warmth and strength of his hand, the cool glide of the lube. My piercings create the perfect ribbed friction I know he craves. His eyes roll back before he shuts them tight, biting his bottom lip.

As I watch, I see his hand twist over our tips. My gaze catches on the thin line of black ink banding around his left ring finger. It's the only tattoo on his body. His permanent wedding ring. A sign of the vows he'll never break. To me. To Hurricane. To Mars and our boys.

He's mine. He's *ours*.

I grab him by the shoulders, pressing my lips to his. We

kiss feverishly, our bodies trembling as he keeps working his fist over our cocks. I bury my tongue in his mouth, opening him deep, sucking on his lip. His skin is so warm against mine, his hair still damp.

"Fuck—daddy, please," he groans, his hand slowing on our dicks.

I smile against his lips. "Do you need to come, angel? Are you aching with it?"

"Yes."

I drop my hand down, slapping his wrist to make him let go of our dicks. "Not yet. You're gonna take that pounding first. I'm gonna fill this ass. Gonna make you bend over and spread wide as I bury my cock so deep you see stars."

"Yes," he says again. "Fucking do it. Cay, I *need* it—"

"You don't come until I say," I command. "I'm gonna fill this ass as you fill my hand. You'll walk out of here King of the Ice with my cum dripping down your thighs."

He's already turning, eager for more. He hands me the lube packet over his shoulder, his hands gripping to the shelves.

I make quick work of tearing it open and squeezing a little onto my fingers. "Bend over," I growl. "Show me what's mine."

He widens his stance, bending at the waist. God, he has a great ass. I smooth my left hand over the thick curve of it. And because I can't fucking help myself, I drop to one knee behind him, burying my face in his heat.

"Oh—*fuck*—Cay—" He's not big into eating ass, but if I'm the one offering, he can't bend over fast enough.

I make a mess of him, swiping with my tongue, getting his hole wet with my spit. He pants, pressing back against my pressure, moaning into the curve of his arm as I suck and tease, rimming his tight hole with my tongue.

"You want this cock, you better relax," I order, nipping the cheek of his ass with my teeth.

He groans again, letting out a shaky breath. "Feels so fucking good."

From my knees, I have the perfect view as I sink one finger into his tight hole.

"God—"

"Breathe," I murmur. "That's it." I work that finger in and out, applying the lube all the way around. His wet heat swallows me and I bite my lip, fighting my own groan. Fuck, I love anal. Very important when you live as part of a bi fourway. I press another finger in, letting them both curl forward and down as I go reaching for his prostate—

"Oh—fuuuuuck," he garbles, breathless and needy.

"Right there?" I tease, working the spot again.

He slams a hand against the shelf, making it all rattle. "*Ungh*—mygod—right fucking there—" His voice is a deep, masculine growl.

I smile, kissing his ass cheek as I press in and down with two fingers, dragging along his prostate until he squirms.

"Baby—*fuck*—daddy, please," he begs. Yeah, his house of cards is crumbling. Play doesn't last long with him before he drops the act and just becomes a feelings machine.

I stand, squeezing the rest of the lube from the packet onto the fingers I still have buried in his ass. Careful not to waste it, I work the lube in. "You ready to take my dick? You gonna be my perfect good fucking boy?"

"Yes," he groans. "God, I love you so fucking much, Cay. Do it."

I pull my fingers free and grip my cock at the base, pressing in close. This first feeling of connection is what I always crave. Whether with Rachel or Jake, it's the first glide home that always takes my breath away.

I press my tip in, letting out a slow exhale. Hearing me, Jake mirrors it and I see his hip muscles relax. I press in deeper, holding my shaft tight as I work in. "God, you're so fucking tight, baby."

He pants a laugh, glancing over his shoulder. "Who's fault is that? How long's it been, Cay?"

"Too fucking long," I reply, sinking in another inch, working in and out all the way to the tip to make sure he's good and stretched. My every instinct is begging me to pound him senseless, but I can't hurt him. I'll die first.

I feel the moment he gives in. His body goes slack and it's suddenly like he's pulling me in as much as I push. "Fu-fu-fuuuuck," he pants, breathless as I sink all the way in.

My hips settle against the curve of his ass and we just pause and breathe, sharing this perfect moment of connection. My hands smooth from his hips, up his sides, over his shoulders. His body is a work of art, honed to perfection.

"You're perfect," I murmur, leaning forward to kiss his warm shoulder. "Perfect."

"I'm perfect now?" he teases, glancing back at me. "You gonna call me King of the—*ahh*—"

I thrust in hard, silencing him with a groan. "Don't fucking push it."

"No, push *me*," he begs. "Fuck me like you're the only one who owns this ass."

"Oh, you want me to pound this ass?" I tease, moving my hips harder against him. "Make you beg. Make you moan—"

"Fuck me, daddy. Please god," he murmurs under his breath. He gives as well as he takes, holding his hips firm as he breathes it out, stifling a groan into the crook of his arm. "Yeah, there—right there—"

I keep one hand on his shoulder, and one on his hip as I

go to town, pounding his tight hole. The sound of our skin slapping fills the room as we groan together, taking our pleasure. "Fuck, you feel so good," I say, ready to give him the praise that will make us both come undone. "You're so beautiful. So strong."

He moans, dropping a hand down to work his cock. "I've missed you," he groans. "Need you. Cay, baby, please—"

His begging has me wrapping myself around him, one hand bracing against his chest as I take over working his cock. "Kiss me," I say. "Jake, kiss me."

He twists himself into a pretzel, keeping his hips locked tight against mine, bending enough to reach my lips as we kiss, our hot breath fanning over each other's lips as we ride out the cresting high of our releases.

"Come with me," I say, my hand working him from tip to base as I rock into his ass with my hips. "Need to feel you come. Squeeze me tight. Take this cock. All of it."

"Fill me, Cay. Make me yours. God—I'm fucking yours," he pants, his ass squeezing me like a vice until I choke back a scream. "Say you love me. Say you need me like I need you. I need you like fucking air, Cay."

I drop my forehead to his back, my thrusting going still as I give him what he needs. "I love you, Jake. You're mine. All fucking mine. My rock and my love, the beating heart of this family. You're the axis that makes our world spin. Be with me forever. Be mine. Jake, please—"

His left hand grabs at mine, weaving our fingers together as he places his on the shelf. His right drops down to wrap around mine on his dick. We work him together as I move my hips once, twice, three more times.

My release barrels through me and I cry out, burying the sound at his back. I come inside him so hard it makes my knees shake. At the same time, he groans beneath me, his hot cum releasing all over our joined hands, dripping in between our knuckles.

"Oh god," he groans.

We hold there, doing nothing but breathe together. This is what he needs. I need the moment when we join. He needs the moment we release. That's when he feels us most in sync. So I wait. I breathe with him. I *be*.

"I love you," I murmur, feeling him relax completely into my hold. "I love you, Jake."

He nods, still too lost in the cloud of his orgasm to reply.

After a moment he lets out a deep breath. His muscles tighten and I know he's back in his own head. "Fuuuuuck, I needed that," he says on a contented sigh. He shifts beneath me and I lift my sticky hand away from his softening dick.

"It was a good shot," I admit at last. "Methodical and clean. You earned it."

He huffs a laugh, glancing over his shoulder. "Come on, it was pretty as a picture and you know it. Fucking textbook."

"It was good," I repeat.

I slip out of him with a grunt, dropping down to pull up my pants. He may have to wear me out of here, but I have to wear him too. Inevitably we'll shower when we get home, which will hopefully morph into round two, preferably with someone with softer curves wedged between us.

Jake pulls up his shorts, one handed, reaching for a roll of paper towel with the other. It's the shit kind they put in the bathrooms, but it's better than nothing. We do the minimum to clean the jizz and lube off our hands.

"You gonna say it now?" he says with a big grin.

"Say what?"

"That I'm a better forward than you."

I glare at him. "You got lucky."

"Nu-uh. No way." He shakes his head, tossing his shirt over his shoulder as he crosses his arms. "You just said it was methodical. You said I earned it."

"I was lying to make you feel better."

"You're such a fucking asshole," he huffs. "Can't you just give me this? One time. One tiny little time, I wanna hear you call me King of the Ice and mean it."

"You're King of the Ice Cream," I reply with a smirk.

"Yes—*wait*—seriously? Ice cream?" His smile turns into a frown.

"What? I thought that was your thing too. Your whole bullshit super power. Remember?"

"It's not bullshit and of course I remember," he replies. "I can be King of two things. Come on, just say it. Say I'm better than you."

Before I can reply, there's a sharp rapping at the door.

Shit...who would knock?

Jake and I exchange a confused look before Ilmari's deep voice calls through the door. "Guys, open the door."

I'm already on the move when I hear Rachel's higher voice, a note of panic in her tone. "Right fucking now!"

I fling my hand out to turn the lock and Rachel pushes the door open. Mars steps in behind her, both babies still zonked out on his chest. Jamie is in the carrier, his legs dangling like limp noodles, while Tuo is balanced in the curl of Ilmari's arm.

"What's wrong?" says Jake, tugging his shirt on. He hands me my hat and I slip it back on.

"I don't know," says Mars, glancing at Rachel. He looks pissed. "She won't tell me. I found her in her office crying. Said we had to come find you."

"I'm not doing this three times," she huffs, glancing

around at the three of us. She looks spun up, my Hurricane incarnate.

"What's wrong, baby?" Jake says again.

Tears well in her eyes as her bottom lip starts to quiver. "At least one of you guys is in really big freaking trouble," she says.

We all share a confused look, and I know their brains are running through the same quick calculus I am. Oh shit, what did we do now?

"Tell us," Ilmari orders.

She lets out a shaky breath through parted lips. "Okay... just know that there's nothing that can be done about it now. I need you all to help me get excited about this, because I'm kind of freaking the fuck out."

"Seattle, please," Jake begs. "Just tell us."

But Hurricane doesn't need to say a word. I already know. All the signs have been there, we've just been too busy to see them. I glance to Ilmari and I know he knows too. His eyes are wide as he glances down at the two babies asleep in his arms.

"Oh, holy shit," Jake gasps, and I know he's finally there too. "Baby, are you—"

"Pregnant," she finishes with him, that bottom lip still quivering. "Yes. *Again*. I've been feeling so tired and weird and—I was wrapping an ice pack around Perry's knee and it just hit me and I knew," she says on one long exhale, dark eyes wide. "But I needed to *know*, you know? I couldn't wait until I got home. So I was in the bathroom freaking out, and Poppy came in, and she had a test in her purse because she thinks she's pregnant too, so she gave it to me and I took it and..."

As if we needed the confirmation, she slips her hand in the front pocket of her Rays fleece and pulls out a little blue-capped pregnancy test. She hands it to me. I glance down, noting the bold blue plus sign looking up at me. I look to Ilmari, holding it up for him to see.

"But...I don't get it," says Jake, glancing from the test back to Rachel. He steps forward, placing his hands on her shoulders, as he searches her face. "Babe...are you...are we not happy about this?"

And that's when she breaks, the tears falling fast and hard. "I didn't want *you* to be unhappy," she cries.

Jake looks like he's just been told they've cancelled ice cream forever. "Rach, what—"

"We've only just gotten used to two. And now I'm knocked up again, and I was so afraid you'd all be mad or sad or-or disappointed. God, I'm a hormonal fucking mess!" She buries her face in her hands and Jake wraps her in his arms.

"Baby, no," he soothes, kissing her brow, her temple, her cheek. "Look at me, Seattle. Look at *us*," he corrects, tipping her chin up.

She sniffles, lifting her gaze to meet ours.

"You're our wife, Rachel," Jake says. "Till death and beyond, baby. You're our whole fucking world. You're really gonna stand here and tell us you're gifting us with another beautiful baby and be worried that we're not gonna appreciate it?"

She sniffs again. "It's stupid. I'm a mess."

"You're pregnant," he teases. "We're used to messy, pregnant Rachel by now."

She graces him with a weak, hiccupy laugh, shaking her head as she wipes beneath her eyes, smudging her makeup.

Jake turns to look at us. "Guys, Rach is pregnant again. Does that change anything for either of you? Either of you looking for an exit?"

"No," I say, as Ilmari vehemently says, "Never."

Rachel nods, eyes still teary as she steps over to Ilmari, taking Tuo from his arms. She tucks him in against her chest, kissing the top of his Rays pom-pom hat. He wiggles, but doesn't wake. She rocks him slowly side to side, her eyes fluttering closed.

I take her in. Her dark hair is piled high in a knot, messy wisps framing her face. The smudge of her eyeliner, the faint circles under her eyes. She works so damn hard. I smile as my gaze settles on her little gold septum ring. When we first met, she kept it out all the time, trying to pretend she was someone she's not. Now she's boldly, unapologetically Rachel Price.

The mother of my children. The woman of my dreams. And she's given me a life so far beyond any of my wildest imaginings.

I step forward, wrapping my arms around her. She breaks at my contact, fresh tears falling. I bend down, kissing first her, then Tuo. "I love you, Hurricane. I love our boys. I love Jake and Mars. And now I love No Name," I add, using the nickname we always give to each new baby.

She makes a sound somewhere between a laugh and a cry, nodding her head.

Jake step in, wrapping his arms around both of us. "And you know I'm in. I love kids. I say we don't stop until we get a full hockey team—"

"No," Rachel and I say together.

Mars steps in on our other side, his large hands braced over Jamie's sleeping back.

"Mars, you in?" Jake says with a raised brow. "Baby number three?"

He nods. "I think I'd like a girl this time...though another boy would also be fine."

"Oh god," Jake says with a snort. "Can you imagine Cay with a girl?" He grins at me. "Shit, I bet you any money it's yours. It's gotta be. Three for three. We each get a baby, and yours will be a moody, gorgeous, potty-mouthed girl."

Rachel smiles up at me, her eyes still watery. "Well, if she's potty-mouthed, at least she'll come by it naturally," she adds, flashing me a knowing look.

Fuck, did Mars rat me out?

"Yeah," I reply, giving her my best asshole smirk. "She gets it from her mom."

THE END

FOR NOW

THANK YOU

Well??? Did you like this not-so-little look into the Happily Ever After of the Price Family? This is only *Volume 1*. I have many more plans to include HEA bonus content as the series grows!

So, if you didn't see the kind of content you were hoping for in this book, I'll beg for your patience. As I build out this universe, I want to leave space for at least a few surprises when it comes to the Price Family, as they will be major side characters in every main book to come.

You will see Rachel and her guys again. And Poseidon. And the Price babies. For now, let's get ready to meet Tess and Ryan.

Oh, and let's thank a few people. Ashley, my alpha reader, I love ya like crazy. To my amazing cohort of loyal betas and loudest cheerleaders—Alex, Amanda, Rachel—your support has meant everything to me.

To Ashley Bennett and Clio Evans—my goddesses— thank you for sharing your sage wisdom. To Sandra Maldo —thank you for being such a joy to create with. I love seeing your covers splashed all over social media! To Sarah Blue— your generosity has been a godsend as I build out my brand.

To my Amazing Facebook Group—the EMILYVERSE is such a wonderful, supportive group of people, and I'm so happy to have each and every one of you on my team.

I want to leave a special 'thank you' here to Jessa Wilder.

We started our indie author journey together. You've cheered for me and mourned with me and counseled me and laughed with me. You've brought me joy, you make me curious, you make me a better writer, and I'm so blessed to call you my friend.

Lastly, to you, my readers. You're the reason I do this. I want to share my stories with you. Thank you for reading.

XO,

Emily

ALSO BY EMILY RATH

SECOND SONS SERIES

Spicy 'why choose' Regency Romance

#1 BEAUTIFUL THINGS

#2 HIS GRACE, THE DUKE

#3 ALCOTT HALL

***

STANDALONES

Contemporary MM Omegaverse

WHISKEY & SIN

***

JACKSONVILLE RAYS SERIES

Spicy Hockey Romance

#0.5 THAT ONE NIGHT

#1 PUCKING AROUND

#2 PUCKING WILD

#3 PUCKING SWEET (Spring 2024)

Additional Stories

LEMONGRASS (Exclusive to the *Queer & Cute Anthology*, coming June 30, 2023)

PUCKING EVER AFTER: VOL 1

PUCKING EVER AFTER: VOL 2 (Coming Winter 2023)

ABOUT THE AUTHOR

Emily Rath is an international bestselling author of romance and fantasy. She lives in Florida with her husband, son, and cat. They regularly comb the local beaches looking for shark teeth.

- Join my FB Group for monthly live sessions, exclusive first looks at art, and chats about ongoing and new projects
- Join my Newsletter to get all major publishing news

Printed in the USA
CPSIA information can be obtained
at www.ICGtesting.com
LVHW022141071023
760447LV00015B/550